The Strange Case of Lorraine Keyes

An Edward Mendez, P. I. Thriller

Book 10

Gerard Denza

The Strange Case of Lorraine Keyes
An Edward Mendez, P. I. Thriller
Book X

 ISBN: 9798884975163

Cover art: Book Covers Art

Also available digitally.

BY THE SAME AUTHOR:

Icarus: The Collected Plays

Ramsay: Dealer of Death

The Edward Mendez, P. I. Thriller Series:
The Time Deceiver
Night Drifter
The Immortal
Target: The Bogeyman
The Deadliest Game
Romo-Ark
Disappearance
The Angel
Doomsday

Cast of Characters:

(in order of appearance)

April Keyes – the younger sister of Lorraine Keyes, who is a mystery on to herself.

Martha King – an innocent bystander who was in the wrong place at the wrong time.

Edward Mendez, P. I. – a shamus who is investigating the Lorraine Keyes murder and an ancient and deadly mystery.

Dottie Mendez – Edward's eldest sister and his secretary and assistant.

Miss Matthews – secretary at the foundling home where Gordon Prentiss stayed. She places her trust in the wrong people.

Ginny Gray – a newspaper woman who knows a good story when she sees one.

Nathalie Montaigne – a Frenchwoman who loves money and doesn't mind taking risks.

Werner Hoffman – a German immigrant who wants the Sumerian urn for himself.

Marlena Lake – a woman well versed in the occult arts. She has more than one secret up her sleeve.

Susan Broder – Marlena's daughter who is practical and level headed and doesn't scare easily.

Irene Wong – a scientist who has an objective interest in the Sumerian urn.

Lt. William Donovan – a competent man who does not disregard the occult.

Alexandra Raymond – works hand in hand with Lt. Donovan as an undercover cop at the 86th Precinct.
Dr. Claire Ingram – medical doctor who likes doing unusual autopsies.
Tom Cooper – a frightened young man who is easily misled.
Jack Dana – a mystery man who warns April Keyes to leave town or else.
Henriette Miller – a librarian who wants to help Edward in his investigation and comes a little too close to the actual crime.
Manuel Mendez – Edward's father and an Adept in the black occult arts.
Ada Lamont – a Las Vegas showgirl who gets herself into a lot of trouble.
Tony Montana – a professional gambler and hood.
Yolanda Estravades – Edward's girlfriend who has just returned from Brazil.
Roger Lee – A Chinese hood who will do just about anything for money.
Nella Mendez – Edward's youngest sister who always gives the best advice even when she's not aware of it.
Detective Marco Morales – good friend of Edward's who likes doing his friend favors. He's a good undercover cop.
Ashton Bennett – Professor Bennett's devoted daughter and a very beautiful woman.
Professor Bernard Bennett – an enigmatic man, learned in ancient history, who plays his cards close to his chest.

Gordon Prentiss – an orphan who may or may not be a murderer.
Brendan Runyon – Manuel Mendez's manservant.
Lorraine Keyes – the murder victim of an unknown assailant.

PROLOGUE

APRIL KEYES finished putting on her new nylon stockings. The young girl felt positively luxurious and very feminine. The nylons enhanced her lovely and slender legs. She slipped her feet into her new black, patent leather pumps. She adjusted the shoulder straps of the navy blue dress. And, as a last and feminine touch, she applied a couple of daubs of Chanel No. 5 just behind the ears.

April looked at herself in the vanity mirror. Nice but not too much...it wasn't a man-trap outfit. She smiled ...something that she hadn't done for a few days...not since her sister's murder.

She picked up the tortoise shell hairbrush and backcombed her blonde, shoulder length hair.

-Okay. I'm ready to meet Mr. Edward Mendez. I hope he's as handsome as his newspaper photos.

April's hand trembled. She put down the hair brush Yes. She was nervous. Meeting strangers was never easy for her. Her sister, Lorraine had been so outgoing. Everyone that she ever met had fallen under her spell. April was more reserved. And, besides, she'd never met a famous ace detective. She didn't know what she was going to say to Mr. Mendez and, yet, she had so much to tell him. Where would she begin? Or should she be the one asking him the questions? After all, aside from her sister's murderer, the detective was the last one to have seen Lorraine alive.

The young girl put down the hair brush and picked up her purse. April shut the lights and left the apartment. She lived on the second floor of a three story apartment building in Brooklyn. It wasn't convenient, but it was all that she could afford. She locked up and was about to descend the stairs...

-Who's there? I know you're down there.

April had seen the figure of a man peering around the corner on the lower floor. The figure of a man pulled back. April heard the cellar door open and close. She was about to hurry out when she heard the third floor apartment door open and close. It was her upstairs neighbor, Martha King; a friendly woman who had just lost her beloved tomcat. April felt sorry for her because she, too, had a soft spot for cats.

-April? Is that you?

-It's me. I was just going out.

Martha King descended the stairs.

-Well, sweetie, if you're headed for the train station and don't mind the company, I'll walk with you.

-I'd love the company.

-Who were you talking to just now?

-I don't know...just some man who I don't think belongs here.

-Have your ever seen him before?

-I didn't get a good enough look at him, but I'm pretty sure that I've never seen him before...at least not around here.

-You're like me. I never forget a face.

The two women walked to the train station. April kept glancing over her shoulder and spotted a man about a half a block away from her and Martha. He was a well dressed man in a business suit.

-Well, here we are. Let's head on up and deposit our tokens and head to the office.

They climbed the stairs that led to the token booth of the elevated train station. They purchased their tokens and waited for the train to pull in. The platform was crowded with early morning commuters. April cautioned her upstairs neighbor.

-Martha, you're standing a little too close to the edge. Move back a little.

Martha didn't respond.

-Martha? Don't you hear me? You're standing too close to the edge.

And, then, to the horror of every onlooker on that train platform, Martha King threw herself in front of the oncoming train.

ONE

DETECTIVE EDWARD Mendez was leaning on the edge of his reception's desk. He was wearing his new navy blue suit and the fit was just a little loose around the waist. He'd lost a little weight recently, but planned on gaining it back at the gymnasium.

-So, Miss April Keyes never showed up.

It was a statement and not a question. Dottie Mendez knew this and simply shrugged her shoulders. Edward continued thinking out loud.

-Makes no sense. She made the appointment which saved me the trouble of going out to Brooklyn to see her.

Dottie jumped into this "conversation."

-Will you go out to her place?

-I've got to. She's a key part of this investigation. I'm assuming she knew here sister better than most. Any information she's got to offer could be important. What time do you have, Dottie?

-Just past eleven. Miss Keyes was due here at nine.

-Then, it's a safe bet-

Before the P. I. could finish that last sentence, Miss April Keyes walked in out of breath and looking quite pale. Edward knew it was her because of the resemblance to her late sister, Lorraine; blonde, shapely and very pretty. April's hair wasn't as long, but it was just as blonde. Edward stood up and greeted the young woman.

-Miss April Keyes?

-Yes. And, I'm so sorry for being so late, but it couldn't be helped. It was just terrible. Terrible! I can't imagine why she did it.

-Let's go into my office and you can tell me all about it. Hey, Dottie? How about some coffee?

-I'll make a fresh pot.

Edward led April Keyes into his office.

-Sit down, Miss Keyes.

-Thanks.

-Mind if I smoke?

-Not at all.

-Cigarette?

-No. Thanks. Lorraine smoked, but I never took it up. She used to tease me about it. She said that it made a woman look more mysterious.

Edward laughed.

-I think your sister was right about that. So, Miss Keyes, what was the terrible thing that delayed you?

-My upstairs neighbor killed herself. Oh, my God! She just threw herself in front of the train. I warned her to move away from the edge. She must have heard me.

-And, she didn't react to your warning?

April Keyes looked directly into Edward's dark, brown eyes.

-No, Mr. Mendez, she didn't. She just stared straight ahead.

-And, then?

-Just leaped on to the tracks.

-Without looking at the train pulling in?

-Yes! It was so odd. It was like...

-Go on. Finish what you were about to say.

-It was like she was in some sort of hypnotic trance.

-Was her behavior strange just prior to this?

-No. Not at all. It wasn't.

Edward took a drag on his cigarette and sat back in his chair.

-Was she depressed this Miss...

-King. Martha King. Now that you mention it, she was. Her cat had just died, but she seemed to be coping all right.

-The police were called in?

-Yes. They came right away, but there wasn't much I could tell them. She was a nice lady, but I didn't really know her all that well.

Edward took another drag on his cigarette.

-Interesting. And, it could lead to something. Might be worth a follow-up, but...that's not why you're here, is it, Miss Keyes?

-No, Mr. Mendez, it isn't. I'm here because of my sister, Lorraine.

Edward put out his cigarette and lit another.

-Yes. Miss Keyes, tell me about Lorraine. Tell me what you've told the police and what you haven't told them. If you hold back anything, I might not be able to help you.

-I won't hold back, Mr. Mendez. Promise. I want to know who killed my sister.

April Keyes took a deep breath. And, at that moment, Dottie walked in and placed a cup of coffee in front of the girl.

-Thanks, Miss...

-Just call me Dottie.

Dottie left the room and closed the door.

Edward took a drag on his cigarette. He waited patiently for Miss Keyes to take the first sip of her coffee.

-Oh, I needed that.

-Good.

-Anyway, I guess I'll start from the beginning...if it is the beginning.

-Take your time.

-Lorraine and I were orphans. Our parents were killed in a car crash out in Jersey City or somewhere near there. We were living there at the time in what must have been a rented house. Lorraine was five and I was just four. It was late June and a beautiful day. I'm still not over it. It was so sudden and unexpected. It turned our lives upside down.

-Tell me about that day.

Lorraine took another sip of her coffee.

-I think our folks were having a hard time of it financially...the Depression and all that. Our Dad was out of work. Well, that morning we had a visitor. He was a tall man and well dressed. Lorraine and I had just finished breakfast and were in the backyard playing. We stopped playing because Lorraine wanted to hear what was going on inside.. She went over to the window and tried peering in. And, for awhile, she just stood there and listened. I thought for sure they were going to find her out, but they didn't. That man left and Lorraine just sat down underneath the window. She looked puzzled, Mr. Mendez, like she couldn't understand what she'd just heard. I walked over to her.

-And, what did your sister overhear?

-The man told our parent to take their car into the city and not to take the two girls...meaning me and Lorraine, I guess.

-Why not?

-Lorraine didn't know. But, she said that our Mom looked really scared.

-Then, what?

-Our Mom called us back into the house and told us not to leave or to let anyone in.

-You mean that they left the two of you alone?

-I know. It doesn't make any sense. Our parents must have been forced into something terrible to leave us alone like that..

Edward nodded and took a drag on his almost spent cigarette.

-Tell me about the car accident.

-I can only tell you what we were told. Lorraine asked all the questions. I was too broken up to even understand what was going on. The cops told Lorraine that it was a head-on collision and that our parents were killed instantly.

-Who hit them? Which vehicle was liable?

-I think my Dad had swerved into the opposing lane and...the people in the other car...don't ask me how...actually walked away from it.

Edward was incredulous.

-Walked away from a head-on collision? Even the driver?

-I think so.

Edward put out his cigarette.

-What else did Lorraine overhear? It must have been more than just to head into the city.

-Lorraine said the man spoke real low and soft.

The P. I. grinned.

-Like a hypnotist would?

-Yes! I think that's what Lorraine must have meant.

-After the accident, Miss Keyes, what happened to you and Lorraine?

-We were placed in an orphanage and-

-And, what?

-Mr. Mendez, this is where my story gets really frightening. We weren't in the orphanage all that long before this couple from some suburb near Jersey City took us in as foster kids. They seemed nice enough. They were a middle-aged couple who had a son of their own and a foster boy. His name was Gordon. He was the foster boy. He was nice.

April took another sip of her coffee, but this time her hand was visibly trembling. Edward offered her a cigarette.

-No. Thanks. I'll be okay.

-You sure about that?

-Yes. We didn't stay there that long...not long at all, really...a week...maybe a little more. And, it was that weekend the murders happened.

-What murders were those? Wait a minute: not the "criss-cross" murders? I remember my sisters' talking about it. It made the headlines for weeks.

-Oh, my God! Yes.

-The two girls and the two boys.

-Mr. Mendez, it was a Saturday and me and Lorraine and Gordon and Tom, their real son, were walking through the woods along these old Indian paths. We were out longer than we should have been and, I guess, Tom's parents came looking for us because when we got back to the house, no one was there. The house was empty.

April took a deep breath.

-Tom, who was about fourteen, I think-

-And, Gordon? How old was he?

-About the same age. I'm really not sure.

-And, what happened next...when you reached the Cooper's home?

-Tom went next door to the neighbors, but they couldn't tell him anything so we just waited around.

-For how long?

-Until it started to get dark. And, that's when Tom called the police. And, you know the rest, I guess, from the papers.

-Let's hear it from you, Miss Keyes.

-The police found them dead in the woods. Their faces were carved with an X slashed from the temple to the jaw. I remember that vividly. They were still alive when it was done and, then, their bodies were hacked to pieces.

-And, the murderer was never caught?

-And, the murderer was never caught. To me, that's the scariest part.

-Okay, Miss Keyes-

-Please, call me April. Miss Keyes sound so formal and cold.

-Fair enough. I'm Edward.

-Edward. That's a nice name.

-How long were the four of you in the house?

-I don't remember. Three or four hours, maybe.

-Were the four of you together all that time?

-I think so. Lorraine and I were afraid to be left alone. The path was narrow and the woods were pretty frightening. At least to me, they were.

-What became of Gordon and Tom?

-I'm not sure, but Lorraine and I went back to the orphanage. I think Gordon did, too. He must have. It was all so confusing to me.

-And, what about Tom?

-He went to live with his grandparents. Lorraine found that out. She was good at that kind of thing. I used to tease her about it. Told her that she ought to join the police force.

Edward leaned forward and placed both palms on his desk.

-What did Lorraine do for a living?

-She was a cosmetics saleslady.

-Freelance?

-No. She worked for some company not too far from here. I think it's called "Masquerade."

-I'll check it out. And, by the way, what was Gordon's last name?

-I don't think I ever knew it.

-But, the Coopers were on the point of adopting him, right?

-That's what he told us. I guess it was true. Why would he lie? What would be the point?

Edward smiled at the pretty girl.

-April, you'd be surprised what people lie about. But, how did this affect you and your sister? All this drama of the murders and going back to the orphanage.

-Well, we never got adopted. I can't believe anyone suspected me and Lorraine of anything to do with the murders. We were just a couple of kids...

-But?

-I think they might have suspected Gordon and maybe even Tom. I really don't know. I was only four years old.

-So, let me ask you this: who would want to kill your sister?

-I don't know.

-Jealous boyfriend, maybe?

-Maybe.

-Who?

-I don't know who she dated. We shared an apartment, but not our personal lives.

Edward placed his hands behind his head. And, he realized that he didn't trust this girl. He said as much.

-I don't believe you, April. Two orphaned sisters clinging to each other all their lives and not sharing secrets...girl secrets. I come from a family of four sisters. Level with me, April

April made ready to leave.

-I told you all I know, Edward. I'm not a liar. I don't know who killed my sister or why he did it. Yes. I'm assuming it was a man.

April Keyes stood up.

-Are we finished?

Edward smiled.

-No. But, you can go. Just one last question? What do you do for a living?

-I'm a private secretary at a publishing house in mid-town.

-Which publishing house?

-"McQueen's." They put out textbooks, mostly.

-Good day, April. And, if you would, just leave your work address and direct phone line with Dottie.

-I will.

April Keyes turned her back on the P. I. and left the office.

Edward waited until the girl had enough time to leave the office building before he walked into the outer office.

-Hey, Dottie? See what you can dig up on a Martha King.

-And, who in hell is Martha King?

-Just some chick who threw herself in front of a moving train this morning.

TWO

EDWARD WALKED back to his office and closed the door. He flipped through the phone directory and found an orphanage located out in Jersey City. It must be the one because there weren't any others listed.

He dialed the main number.

-Jersey City Foundling Home.

-Edward Mendez. I'm a private investigator.

-Yes. I know the name. How may we help you, Mr. Mendez?

-There were two girls under your care who were brought there some fifteen years ago: Lorraine and April Keyes.

-Yes. Very pleasant and well behaved girls. Miss April took a secretarial course with us. She was very apt.

-And, what about her sister, Lorraine?

-A nice girl.

-Yes?

-Lorraine wanted the unattainable things in life that someone in her social position ...well, you do get my drift, don't you?

Edward got her "drift" all right.

-And, your name?

-Matthews. Jessie Matthews. I should have introduced myself. Sorry.

-You do know that Lorraine Keyes has been murdered.

There was a pause on the other end of the line.

-I did not. How dreadful! I'm very sorry to hear it. She was so young and pretty. I'm quite shocked by what you just told me, Mr. Mendez. Really...it is a tragedy.

-I wasn't too subtle, was I?

-How could one be subtle about a thing like that? I take it that you're investigating her murder?

-I am, Miss Matthews.

-Well, if there's anything that I can do to help, I'd be more than willing. It really is too dreadful.

-As a matter of fact, there is. Was a young boy by the name of Gordon at your foundling home?

-What's the boy's surname?

-Not a clue. But, a couple by the name of Cooper were looking to adopt him at about the time the Keyes sisters arrived.

Edward waited for what seemed like a long moment.

-Miss Matthews? You still there?

-Mr. Mendez, you are of course referring to that murdered couple out in New Jersey? The one that the tabloids had such a field day on.

-Yes.

-Hold the wire, please.

Edward held the wire and took out a cigarette.

-Gordon Prentiss. Yes. He was here.

Miss Matthews demeanor had undergone a radical change.

-What happened to Gordon Prentiss?

-After the Coopers had been killed, he was brought back here; but, he didn't stay long. People can be so cruel! He was taken into custody and never brought back.

Edward was incredulous hearing this.

-You mean he was arrested?

-The authorities didn't call it that. He was taken into custody and placed in some boys' institution.

-But, he was arrested on suspicion of murder?

-I wasn't privy to the details. Gordon was taken in the dead of night. I wasn't on duty at the time.

-Who was?

-That person is long gone. Sheila Whit was her name and not a very dependable person. You wouldn't get very far with her, I'm afraid.

-Miss Matthews, thanks so much. I might be dropping by some time. Just a friendly warning.

-I'll look forward to meeting you, Mr. Mendez. And, Mr. Mendez, Gordon was a nice and quiet boy. His parents had been killed in some kind of auto accident. My other line is ringing. I must go.

-Hey, Dottie? I'm heading for Masquerade Cosmetics.

-If they're giving away free samples, I'll take a few.

Edward got into his DeSoto and drove the half mile uptown. He found a parking spot right in front of Masquerade Cosmetics. He walked into a small reception area and asked to speak to the manager. A man of about sixty came out and greeted the P. I.

-May I help you?

-Edward Mendez.

-A pleasure. Now, how can I help you?

The P. I. got straight to the point.

-Did a Miss Lorraine Keyes work here?

-I don't know the name. She a friend of yours?

-Was.

-Oh? You break up with her? Lover's quarrel?

-She was murdered.

-My God. I didn't mean to sound so off-handed.

-No one by that name ever worked here? You sure of that?

-Definitely not, Mr. Mendez. I know all our girls. I train them.

-Maybe she used another name. She was blonde and about five foot four with a slim figure. She liked black dresses and high heels.

-I would remember such a creature. I'm afraid that I'm unable to help you.

Edward smiled at the rather effeminate man who hadn't bothered to give his name.

-You have helped me, pal.

April Keyes or her deceased sister was a liar.

Edward was back in his office. He was on the phone to Ginny Gray, newspaper woman.

-Hey, Ginny? Edward Mendez.

-Hey, Eddie. What's up?

-Do you recollect about fifteen years ago the "criss-cross" murders out in New Jersey?

-You bet. Even made the New York headlines. Only not so much the murders which were pretty ghastly, but the suspects.

-Two twelve year old boys.

-Close. The elder one was fifteen and the main suspect. The younger boy was fourteen.

-Tom Cooper and Gordon Prentiss.

-Reverse that and you've got it right. Case is still officially unsolved. And, weren't there two girls in that loop?

-Lorraine and April Keyes.

-Lorraine Keyes? The one who just got herself murdered? Hey, Eddie, I'm starting to smell a story here. Give.

-April Keyes is a client of mine...sort of.

-Why am I not surprised?

Edward laughed into the receiver and lit a cigarette.

-So, Eddie, you think Lorraine Keyes' past had something to do with her murder? Sounds like a long shot to me, but people's past do sometimes catch up with them.

-I'm used to long shots. Ginny, can you dig up any newspaper clips for me? Were any arrests made – any suspects rounded up – the motive for the killings – the Coopers' background? Were they "clean" or shady? You know, the easy stuff.

-I'm on it.

-And, Ginny, it's motive I'm looking for. Why were they bumped off? Was it a random killing by some psychopath who never struck again or was it something a lot darker than that.

-Eddie, you make murder sound *so* intriguing.

Edward took a drag on his cigarette.

-By the way, Ginny, will I see you at the exhibition tonight? You know...some Sumerian artifacts about six thousand years old.

-I'll try and make it. I wangled an invitation for me and my new camera man, Carl. But, Edward, things have been hectic around here. There's been a lot of talk about Egypt.

-Like what?

-It's just a bit hush hush, but it's got to do with air defense. Keep that under your belt.

-I will. Hope you can make it tonight.

THREE

-I DO not want to be late, Werner. I am so looking forward to this exhibition. You see? Your enthusiasm has been contagious.

-We've plenty of time, Nathalie. I like your outfit, by the way. Tasteful, but not conspicuous.

-And, your pin-stripe suit is quite appropriate. I hope the guests will be interesting. Boring people can be quite tiresome.

-I wonder if any of the pieces will be available for purchase? Not tonight, of course, but hints can be dropped to the appropriate people.

-It is the urn that you desire, cherie. Tell Nathalie the attraction.

-I like the sound of it.

-What do you mean?

-Its vibration. Its essence and structure.

-Still, I do not understand.

-I must touch it to make certain of its authenticity. Just think of it, Nathalie, an artifact that is nearly six thousand years old! It has survived through the millennia. It is a traveler of space and time. And, I must have it.

-Calm yourself, dear Werner. We must get to the exhibit hall first, no?

-Of course. I must discipline myself. Forgive the outburst.

-Forgiven and forgotten.

Marlena Lake glanced at the hall clock. It was a late 19th century Grandfather clock that she had purchased upon the death of her late husband. It was a purchase that was meant to signify the forward movement of time. The time read 5:30 P. M. Edward was to arrive at 6 P. M. to escort Marlena and her daughter, Susan and their house guest, Irene Wong, to the Sumerian exhibit at the Museum of Natural History. Marlena was rather thrilled by the prospect of seeing the artifacts...artifacts of a civilization that she found intriguing and quite mysterious. She, herself, possessed a Sumerian amulet that had once been used in a rather dramatic and deadly ceremony in Egypt. The amulet would be left at home, of course, in the wall safe in the library.

Marlena walked into her living room. She was wearing an expensive black dress and black pumps purchased from Selby's. It was where she purchased all her shoes...style and subtle taste. She went to the drinks table and poured herself a drink: Chivas Regal on the rocks. She would limit herself to one drink...well, perhaps, two. Edward would want a drink before leaving for the exhibit. And, what in the world was keeping Susan? It wasn't like her daughter to be dawdling.

Marlena heard footsteps on the stairs. She recognized her daughter's footfall.

-I'm in the living room, Susan.

Susan Broder walked in and nodded to her mother. Marlena approved of her daughter's attire: a dark green dress that reached below the knee and black pumps. The young girl also wore a long stranded necklace that spoke of expensive costume jewelry.

-Mother, I think I'll pour myself a drink while we're waiting for Edward and Irene.

-Excellent idea. I'm enjoying one myself. Where is Irene by the way?

-Still primping, I imagine. It takes me no time at all to get ready.

-I like your ensemble, dear. It rather screams good taste. And, your perfume is exquisite, as always.

Susan poured herself a drink.

-I hope Edward isn't late.

-If he is, I'm sure it's for a good reason.

-His work?

-Of course.

-I did tell him to come alone, you know.

Susan smiled.

-You mean not to bring his new girlfriend along?

-Frankly, I don't like her. Yolanda is gone and good riddance to the bitch. Perhaps, she'll even get lost somewhere in the Amazon.

-I think this Jamie Farley is an infatuation. He couldn't have gotten over Yolanda so quickly.

-Who cares about her? She was a nuisance.

Susan thought it wise to change the subject before Irene came downstairs and Edward arrived.

-Mother? Who's sponsoring this Sumerian exhibit?

-I've no idea. I was going to ask you. You're so good at finding things out.

-I guess we'll find out when we get there.

Irene Wong descended the staircase wearing a midnight blue Mandarin dress that molded to her exquisite figure. The perfume she was wearing was more exotic and alluring than Susan's. Her make-up was carefully applied with special attention paid to her eyes. She was about to enter the living room when the doorbell rang. She went to answer it.

-Irene! You look lovely...really lovely.

-Thank you, Edward. And you look very handsome. Please come in. I think Marlena and Susan are in the living room. I just came down.

Irene led the way into the living room.

-Edward, dear boy, you're a trifle early. I approve. Please, have a seat. Susan will mix you your usual whiskey and soda. Won't you, dear?

-Thanks, Marlena. I could use a drink. Hello, Susan.

Edward sat down next to Marlena on the sofa. Irene sat in the armchair opposite them and crossed her beautiful legs. Susan handed Edward his drink and, then, fetched a club soda for Irene.

-So, Marlena, what's your interest in this artifact exhibition.

-Curiosity?

-Try, again.

-You know me too well, Edward. These objects on display...some are said to even predate the Sumerian civilization.

-Marlena?

-Yes, Irene?

-Could you tell us a little bit about the Sumerians and about the city of Sumer, itself? I know so very little of that civilization.

-Why of course, dear.

Edward finished his drink.

-I could use a little education myself on that subject.

Edward turned to Susan.

-Susan, what about you? I bet you could teach us a thing or two.

-I'll let my mother start things off. Mother?

-Don't be impertinent.

-It was simply an introduction. Marlena began her brief lecture.

-The Sumerian civilization seems to have sprung from literally nowhere. As of this date, no previous epoch has been discovered. It was circa 4,000 B.C. that

Sumer, the capital city, made its appearance...and its appearance was that of a highly sophisticated and complex culture. Theirs was the first known written language. They had a code of ethics and a judicial system that exceeded our own. The Sumerians were advanced in all areas of the arts and sciences. They had the rudiments of algebra and advanced mathematics. Yet, their origins remain a mystery. They were researchers into the occult arts. Their gods were said to be more than mere legends and myth.

Edward took out a cigarette and lit up.

-Too bad they had nasty neighbors who must have conquered and exploited them.

-Yes. A great pity, that. Anyway, I think it's time we were on our way.

Marlena and company were the first to arrive at the museum. The Security Guard escorted them into the exhibit hall. The artifacts were displayed on long tables and without the protection of glass cases. Edward commented on this.

-That's strange. Leaving priceless artifacts lying about.

Marlena also wondered about this.

-It is tempting fate. A very foolish and careless act. I must speak to the museum curator about this.

Irene and Susan had wandered off to examine the artifacts: vases, jewelry, rather odd but beautiful figurines. They stopped to examine one particular statuette.

-Enlil.

-Susan?

-He's their god, Enlil, the founder of their civilization. Well, he and his brother, Enki.

-Where did Enlil come from?

-He descended from the heavens.

For some reason, Susan found herself fascinated by the statue. Irene noticed this.

-Susan, how intently you stare at the Sumerian god.

-I wonder if he were actually a man who once existed.

-I'm sure he was a gifted genius ahead of his time. Or-

-Yes?

-A visitor from another world or dimension; a personage who we would consider a god.

-My mother would agree with you on that theory, Irene.

-And, you don't?

-I'm not sure.

Other visitors were entering the exhibit hall. Werner Hoffman and Nathalie Montaigne were among them.

-Werner, look over there. It's Edward Mendez. And, I believe that's Marlena Lake with him. Perhaps, we should leave, this could be awkward.

-No. We are not leaving, my dear. I seem to have a vague memory of meeting him at one time. Come. We'll introduce ourselves to the private investigator.

-As you wish.

The two people approached Edward and Marlena.

-Mr. Mendez, I am Werner Hoffman and this is my good friend, Miss Nathalie Montaigne. Have we met before tonight? It is an odd question, but I must ask it of you.

Edward smiled at the stern looking man and his companion who was wearing too much make-up.

-Yes and no, Mr. Hoffman. Don't mean to be so mysterious, but the explanation for my cryptic answer would be lengthy and complex.

-We must save it for another time, then.

In the meantime, Nathalie had wandered off in search of the Sumerian urn that Werner had mentioned. She found it and called over to her companion.

-Werner! Pardon me for interrupting, but I have found the urn that you so often have spoken of.

-Excellent! Mr. Mendez? Miss Lake? Please excuse me.

Werner Hoffman made his apologies to Edward and Marlena and rushed over to where Nathalie stood.

More visitors were entering the exhibit hall and among them was Lt. William Donovan dressed in plain clothes. He was escorting Alexandra Raymond who was also in plain clothes. Edward recognized them at once and waved them over.

-Hey, Bill? Alex? Over here.

The Lieutenant and Alex joined Edward and Marlena.

-Well, hello Lieutenant-

Lt. Donovan cut of the P. I.

-Just call me Bill.

-Got ya'. Alex? How have you been?

-Pretty darn good. And, you, Edward? What case are you working on? No. Let me guess: the Lorraine Keyes murder. And, that was an educated and professional guess.

Lt. Donovan smiled.

-Translation: she knew.

-Tattle-tale.

Edward looked around for Ginny Gray, but couldn't spot her.

And, near the Sumerian urn...

-Werner, it doesn't really look like much, but...

--Go ahead, Nathalie.

-It's quite thick and the color... I can't place the exact shade...blue...gray...or even a subtle shade of black?

-Don't try.

Werner Hoffman made to touch the ancient object.

-Werner, you should not handle it.

-Why not? It's survived over 6,000 thousand years of existence. Will my hand tarnish it?

Having made that statement, he touched the outer perimeter of the urn.

-My God! Nathalie, can you feel the vibration in the very air?

In point of fact, the Frenchwoman *did* feel something...a change in the air...a charge of electricity.

-Werner, let it go. I do feel something rather unsettling.

Werner Hoffman ignored her warning. He placed his hand along the inner rim of the urn and the vibration increased. He began to move his hand along that rim causing the urn to move...to rotate upon itself.

-My God! Werner, stop! The sound is increasing.

Werner Hoffman did not stop. He could not stop. His right hand was now rotating the urn more and more rapidly upon itself. The urn was fast becoming a blur of color and motion. People near to Werner and Nathalie turned to look and see where the sound...the ethereal "music" was coming from.

The urn's rotation increased. Werner Hoffman could not release his hand from the rotating prison. He was unable to use any part of is body save that right hand. He wanted to scream, but could not. He stared straight ahead as a man transfixed, but who could see nothing. The vibrating pitch now reached the ears of Edward Mendez and his friends.

-What the hell is that sound...that vibration? It's deafening. Christ!

Everyone in the hall made to cover their ears. The sound was starting to become unbearably painful. Nathalie Montaigne was on the point of screaming.

-Werner! For God's sake- stop it or I will go insane!

She was afraid to touch the object which had now become a blur of motion.

-Werner! Can you hear me, cherie? Let go of the damned thing. Stop! I beg of you!

Werner Hoffman no longer had the capacity to hear his companion. He'd been rendered deaf and senseless.

Marlena saw where the sound was coming from and acted instantly.

-Edward, it's over there where that urn was. Stop it from rotating or we'll all be killed or worse. Look! It's Werner Hoffman. Hurry, Edward, if it's not already too late.

The P. I. didn't need to be told the gravity of the situation. He started for where Werner Hoffman stood. Irene pointed to the window.

-Susan...Marlena...the glass is starting to shatter. We must leave this place at once.

Marlena agreed.

-That urn is a weapon and that fool, Hoffman, has unleashed its power.

Edward had reached Hoffman as every window in the gallery shattered. The P. I. kicked the display table on its underside dislodging the urn's hold on Hoffman. The urn went clattering across the floor for a short distance. Those people who hadn't fled the gallery quickly recovered except for Werner Hoffman.

Edward bent over to examine the German. Nathalie stood over the two men.

-Mr. Mendez, is he dead?

-He's breathing, but-

-Yes? Do not spare me.

-His eyes.

-Eh? What about them?

-They're turned completely in. It's as if he were dead.

FOUR

EDWARD MENDEZ, P. I. was standing in the morgue of Roosevelt Hospital in Manhattan's upper east side. Dr. Claire Ingram was standing opposite him with the empty metal tray that had contained Werner Hoffman.

-So, where is he? I thought he was dead.

-Not quite, Mendez. Although, he'd be far better off if he were.

-How's that doctor?

-What did you have for lunch, Mendez?

-Tuna on rye. And, what the hell does that have to do with anything?

-Was there lettuce that came with that sandwich?

-Yes...

-Well, Mendez, that slice of lettuce has more brain power than Werner Hoffman.

-You mean he's as good as brain dead?

-That's a difficult question to answer.

-Give it a try.

-Come with me to his room. You'll get a better idea of what I'm trying to explain to you...and to myself.

And, in an isolated section of the Critical Care Unit located on the ninth floor...

-Why the hell is he in restraints?

Edward asked this question staring down at the body of Werner Hoffman whose hands and feet were strapped down. The man's eyes were open, but the eyes were unfocused and all the color had drained from them.

-He's a danger to himself and others.

-I'm not following you, Doctor. Just how is a lettuce leaf dangerous?

-His brain has been rendered into a mass of jelly and liquid. He should be dead or completely senseless. The cranium is on the point of shattering into dust and when that happens he will certainly be dead. The brain matter will literally start dripping out of him.

-Christ!

-I'm not quite finished. Several times, Mr. Hoffman has tried to rise and each time he tried to actually bite the attendant.

-What the hell are you saying?

-Whatever remains in the skull has reduced him to cannibalism at worst or homicidal tendencies at best for lack of a better term. He'll have to be put away after they're through with examining him. Putting it bluntly, his case is hopeless in the extreme.

Before the P. I. could react to these statements, Dr. Ingram had a few questions for him.

-What's happened to the urn, Mendez? Have the police confiscated it? They must have for the public's safety.

-Lt. Donovan took charge of it. I guess. I rode in with the ambulance. That urn's some kind of a weapon..

-Quite. And, Mendez?

-What?

-You look distracted. Working on that Lorraine Keyes case, I've heard. Any progress?

-Some. It's still pretty early on.

-Correct me if I'm wrong, but are you attempting to connect "dots?"

-You could say that, Doctor Ingram.

-You don't think that this Sumerian urn and Miss Keyes' demise are connected in any way, do you?

-My P. I. gut instinct says that they just might be.

-But, how?

The P. I. shook his head.

-Beats me. But, I've got a lot of loose dots that need connecting.

-Was Miss Keyes involved in antiques? That would explain the connection.

-It could explain a lot of things.

-Keep me posted, will- Oh!

Werner Hoffman was struggling to free himself.

-Dr. Ingram- Claire! For God's sake look at his face.

All humanity had drained from the features of Werner Hoffman. His teeth were stained yellow, saliva dripped from his open mouth and-

-He's chewing his damned tongue!

Dr. Ingram rang for help. Edward stood back and wondered what this all meant...what it meant to his case on Lorraine Keyes and what it meant to humanity at large.

Help arrived and tongue depressors were applied to Hoffman along with heavy sedation. But, Dr. Ingram had her doubts about any medication being effective. Edward said his goodbyes and rushed from the ghastly sight: a man had been transformed into some kind of hideous ghoul.

The P. I. got into his DeSoto and headed for the 86th Precinct.

-So, what happened to the damned thing? I thought you had it.

-Beats the hell out of me. Me and Alex had to call for back-up and keep everyone inside that exhibit gallery. The last I saw, you were kicking it out of Hoffman's hand.

-And, it landed where? I didn't have any time to notice. I was too busy with Herr Hoffman which turned out to be a waste of time. The guy's ready for the vegetable bin or an insane asylum; take your pick.

Lt. Donovan shook his head. He looked across his desk at Edward.

-We've gotta' assume that it fell to the floor.

-Okay. I'm with you on that.

-And, someone picked it up.

-A pretty dangerous thing to do, Lieutenant.

-I'll say! So who took off with it? Any guesses, Mendez?

-Yes. I can think of only one person with enough gall and guts to take that urn.

-Give. I mean it, Mendez. I don't like guessing games.

-Miss Marlena Lake.

Lt. Donovan slapped himself on the forehead.

-Yes! That woman's got balls!

-My mother... Do you realize that you've just committed a criminal offense? It could even be considered a felony.

-I'll speak with the museum people, eventually.

Irene addressed Marlena.

-Miss Lake, that object may be quite dangerous. Look what it did to Mr. Hoffman.

-Hoffman was a fool. The urn must be studied and examined under the most stringent scientific conditions. Yes. I agree with you, Irene. It is dangerous and, perhaps, far more than we realize. But, how terribly thrilling it all is!

-The police might have a different opinion about all this. They might be knocking on our front door soon.

-No one knows that I absconded with it. I was quite careful in procuring it.

-You mean stealing it?

-You're starting to bore me, young lady.

Miss Wong interrupted.

-Marlena, why not put it in your wall safe for at least the time being. It shouldn't be handled or carried about haphazardly.

-Capital idea, Irene. Susan, here, place it in the wall safe for mother.

Susan drew back.

-Forget it! I'm not touching that thing and neither should you. Just shove your purse into the wall safe and be done with it.

-Coward. I'll place it there myself. Mix me a drink while I'm gone, will you.

Marlena left the room with pocketbook in hand.

-My mother...

-Don't be too hard on her, Susan. As a scientist, I'm most curious to examine that urn. We shouldn't be deceived by its outer casing, though. What lies hidden within that structure, I wonder. It is obviously not an urn, but a weapon or something even more staggering.

-I'll get the drinks. I sure could use one.

Susan was not won over by Irene's enthusiasm. That urn belonged to someone who would be looking for it. And, was Werner Hoffman simply touching it out of curiosity or was he trying to steal it? That answer would never come from Werner Hoffman, himself, but maybe Nathalie Montaigne might know.

Susan was at the drinks table and happened to look up. At the window was a face peering in...a cold and hard face of a man whose eyes focused on her with such malice that the girl did something quite out character. She screamed in fear and dropped the bottle of Scotch to the floor.

FIVE

EDWARD MENDEZ drove the short distance from the 86th Precinct to Marlena Lake''s townhouse. It was 2 A.M., but the P. I. felt certain that Marlena was awake and up to her usual antics. Traffic heading uptown was light at this time of day. Edward popped a piece of bubble gum into his mouth. It was his way of cutting back on smoking two packs a day. He'd eventually get it down to just one pack. He had no intention of giving up his Lucky Strikes. He liked the flavor of tobacco and the cigarettes helped steady his thoughts. He also liked blowing smoke in people's faces of whom he didn't like. It helped with the interrogation process.

Edward pulled on to Marlena's street. His headlights illuminated her front door and the man who was lurking near her living room window.

-Now, who the hell is that?

The P. I. pulled into a parking space and jumped out of his DeSoto.

-Hey, you! Get over here!

The man ran in the opposite direction and was lost in the dark. Edward put his Waltham back into its holster and walked over to the front door which was swung open by Marlena. She was holding a loaded pistol in her hand.

-Edward, dear boy.

-Marlena, baby, I just spotted a prowler out here.

-Yes. Susan saw a man...a rather old man...peering through the window just now. Do come in.

Edward was shown into the library.

-We've much to discuss. Susan and Irene are in my daughter's bedroom upstairs behind a locked door. That prowler gave Susan quite a fright.

-And, Susan doesn't scare too easily, does she?

-No. She doesn't. She said that there was something familiar about that face, but she couldn't quite place it.

Edward rubbed his clean shaven chin.

-You know, Marlena, now that you mention it, there *was* something familiar about that character.

-Can you be more specific, Edward? Susan couldn't.

-The way he carried himself and his posture...he didn't have a limp, but he was having difficulty walking even though he moved pretty fast. Didn't get a good look at his face, though.

-Not your common prowler. Anyway, what brings you to my domicile at this time of the morning?

-You know why I'm here.

-Do I?

-Don't be coy with me, Marlena. The urn from the museum that you pocketed.

-Oh, that.

-It could be considered grand theft.

-Impossible.

-What are you up to?

-Why nothing at all. But how can one steal what one already owns?

-You don't mean to say that you own that thing?

-Yes, Edward. It was I who sponsored that exhibit of Sumerian objects. It was I who placed the appropriate bait to catch the proverbial mouse.

-Werner Hoffman.

-Precisely. I knew that that particular urn predated even the Sumerian civilization, but was it a weapon or a homing device.

-A homing device for where?

-Don't interrupt, dear boy. Or was its use for something undreamed of?

-How did you find out about it?

-You forget, Edward, that I am a collector of religious and ancient artifacts.

-I seem to recall you pilfering a few holy items. Yes.

-Yes. Well, that urn was among my collection. I had to find out the extent of its powers. And, tonight, I saw what it could do. Rather frightening, wouldn't you say?

-Are you frightened, Marlena?

-Much more curious than frightened.

-Better be careful with it. Look what it did to Hoffman.

-Rendered him senseless, it seems.

-You wouldn't know then.

-What's happened to the man? I must know.

-His brain is a mass of jelly. He's less than a vegetable.

Marlena took a deep breath.

-And, if it had gone on unchecked...dear boy, you may have saved us all.

-What do you plan on doing with that urn?

-It must be examined under the strictest of conditions.

-By whom?

-Why myself, of course, and possibly Irene and Professor Bernard Bennett, the famous archaeologist..

-Well, you better let Lt. Donovan in on your plans. And, by the way, can you prove ownership, Marlena?

-Of course. It cost me enough.

-Who'd you get it from?

-From the man who you and I defeated three years ago; my former lover, the ancient one.

SIX

EDWARD WAS back in his office, but not for long, not having gotten too much sleep. He had to track down Gordon Prentiss and Tom Cooper: two young men who could be murderers in an unsolved case going back some fifteen years. He got ready for the short trip to Jersey City. Dottie had located Tom Cooper. He'd moved back to New Jersey and had purchased the same house that he and his parents had once lived in. She'd also done her research on Martha King. Nothing extraordinary to report there: a working class woman who hailed form Indianapolis. Had lived in New York these past ten years, no criminal record.

The P. I. stepped out into the street and just had time to glimpse a man...a very old man...dashing out of sight.

-I'll be damned. He's tailing me. Well, let him.

Edward got into his DeSoto and drove out to Jersey City. There wasn't much of a downtown area, but that part of town wasn't his destination. He drove three miles into that city's suburb and stopped right in front of a two story, green clapboard house. It looked like it had been built sometime in the 1920's. It was sturdy with no exterior trimmings.

The P. I. got out of his car and walked on to the porch. He rang the doorbell. It was immediately opened by a young man in his late twenties. He was tall and lean and had an athletic build. His manner was hesitant...bordering on frightened.

-Yes? What can I do for you?

-Edward Mendez. I'm a private investigator, Mr. Cooper.

-Tom Cooper. You wanna' come on in?

Tom Cooper had a thick New Jersey accent.

-Thanks.

Edward stepped into a dimly lit corridor that lead into an equally dimly lit parlor with modern furniture.

-Nice place you've got here, Mr. Cooper.

-Call me Tommy. Have a seat. I don't get too many visitors.

-A young man like yourself...why not?

-I'm not so young. I'm thirty...or will be.

-Old enough to remember fifteen years back?

-You mean my parents' murder? Sure. I remember that. How could I forget it?

-Tommy, do you remember two young girls who stayed here at that time?

Tom Cooper actually smiled.

-Sure. Lorraine and April. They were nice. I liked them.

-You know that Lorraine Keyes was murdered.

-I read about it in the papers. You after her killer?

-That's my job.

-Am I a suspect, Mr. Mendez? The last time I saw Lorraine was just about fifteen years ago.

The P. I. nodded.

-Tommy, what about Gordon Prentiss?

-What about him?

-Have you kept in contact?

-No. No reason to.

Edward noted the abrupt change in Tom Cooper's manner. He had begun to relax during their conversation, but he was now tense and defensive.

-Did you like Gordon?

-Yes.

That was not a convincing answer.

-Your parents wanted to adopt him.

-Maybe.

-Maybe?

-It never happened.

-They were killed.

-Murdered.

-Tommy, do you remember anything out of the ordinary on that day?

Tom Cooper got up and walked over to the bay window.

-It was all so unreal whenever I look back on it.

-How so?

-Me and Gordon took the girls for a hike in the woods. They wanted to go. They pretty much begged us. We left here about nine in the morning and might've stayed out later than we should have. Nothing happened out there. We walked along the Indian paths and stopped now and then to rest. We lost track of time, I guess. We got back later than we should have...a lot later.

-What time was that?

-Maybe after three in the afternoon.

-Tommy, that was a six hour hike. The girls were only five years old.

-We lost track of time, like I said. I don't know how it happened.

-And, your parents had gone out to look for you.

-I guess they were worried about the girls. Me and Gordon could look after ourselves.

Edward shook his head. Tommy continued with his story.

-Me and Gordon were suspects, I know that. Mr. Mendez, I didn't kill my folks. No way in Heaven and Earth could I do a thing like that. I don't know who did it. I don't.

-Did Gordon kill them?

-He couldn't have. He was with us the whole time, practically.

-"Practically?"

-He scouted ahead every now and then, but I never lost sight of him. He-

-What, Tommy? Tell me.

-He made these kinds of bird calls, but it sounded like no bird I ever heard.

-Did Gordon have any visitors?

-No. Foster kids don't get visitors.

-What about phone calls?

-None that I know of.

-Did he ever leave the house on his own?

-Sure. To the candy store, drugstore. You know, stuff like that.

-Where is he now?

-Beats me, Mr. Mendez.

-Sure you don't know where he is?

-Why should I?

-Tommy, I hope you're leveling with me.

-I don't know what you mean by that.

-I think you do. Mind if I light up?

-Go ahead. I don't smoke, myself.

-Thanks.

Edward reached into his jacket pocket for his pack of Lucky Strike.

-Anything else you want to know, Mr. Mendez?

-No. Can't think of anything else. Can you?

-Nope.

Edward lit up and took his leave of Tommy Cooper. The door closed behind the P. I. and Edward caught the face of Tommy Cooper looking furtively through the slats of the Venetian blinds.

-Well, Ginny?

-Nothing. Gordon Prentiss has done a vanishing act.

-When the hell did he "vanish?"

-The day after he left the foundling home. Zap! Like a puff of proverbial smoke.

Edward sat back and popped a piece of bubble gum into his mouth.

-People don't just vanish, Ginny. He's somewhere. And, according to Miss Matthews, he was taken from the foundling home in Jersey sometime in the middle of the night.

-He was relocated, Eddie, but I can't find out where. Those records are sealed tighter than a too tight girdle. And, he probably has nothing to do with Lorraine Keyes' murder.

-Meaning, I oughta' focus on the present day events and people?

-Yes.

-You might be right, but it's a loose end and I don't like loose ends.

-What's the scoop on Mr. Tom Cooper?

-He's holding out on me, big time. I'll have to pay him another visit and rattle him.

-What about April Keyes? She oughta' know something.

-That's another holdout.

-And, to drastically change the subject, fill me in on that museum debacle. I couldn't make it to the exhibition...this Egyptian business is heating up.

Edward told Ginny everything including Marlena's part in it.

-So, Ginny keep the lid on Marlena's part in this for the time being. I want to see what she has up her sleeve.

-Deal...for now. And, Eddie, take the advice of a woman journalist: keep pumping Miss April Keyes.

-I do have a slight lead on Lorraine's boyfriend.

-You mean her killer?

-I think they're one and the same. That's usually the case.

-You happen to be right about that. So who is he? Give, baby.

-A hitman with Romo-Ark.

-Oh, brother!

-So, Ginny, any contacts in that nefarious firm?

-As a matter of fact, two contacts: a young woman and man.

-Names?

-Rob Barton who works – used to work – down in the mail room And, Liz Fulton, one of their PBX operators; fancy name for a telephone operator. She's good and sharp, Eddie. So, is Rob who's a bit of a bohemian. You'll like him.

-Come to think of it, where has Romo-Ark relocated to?

Ginny reached for her index file.

-Here it is: 50th St. right off of 3rd Ave. A real steel and glass skyscraper, not so tall, a mere forty stories.

-Tall enough for a convenient suicide jump.

Ginny laughed

-Please! And, keep me posted, Mr. Private Eye.

-Naturally.

-And, what's with the bubble gum? Give me a piece, will you?

SEVEN

APRIL KEYES had taken the morning off from work. She had had a night out with a couple of girlfriends and was suffering from a hangover...just one too many cocktails. She should have known better. She was just getting out of bed when a sharp knock on the door drove the hangover right out of her head.

-Oh, my God!

April composed herself enough to respond.

-Who is it?

-Open up. We've gotta' talk.

-Hey, pal, just who are you?

-Jack Dana.

-Who? I don't know any Jack Dana.

-You heard me, sister. Now, open up or I break this door in.

-Why don't you just beat it?

-One last time...open up! It's about you and your late sister.

April got up from the bed, pulled on her bathrobe and went to open the door.

-I'm not dressed.

-You're decent enough.

Against her better judgment, April took the safety chain off the door and let the stranger in. She moved away from the door and sat on the edge of her bed. The stranger stepped into her apartment.

-Good. This won't take long.

Mr. Jack Dana was tall: six foot two. He had an unmistakable athletic built. He was a man in his mid-thirties. He was wearing a black suit with a white collar shirt and no tie. April noticed that a pair of sunglasses was tucked into his outer jacket pocket.

-You're not to see or communicate with that private dick, Edward Mendez.

He was silent for a moment waiting for April's response.

-You threaten to knock down my door just to tell me that?

-Keep out of your later sister's affairs. Believe me, you didn't know your sister.

-Why should I listen to you?

-Because if you don't, I'll have to kill you.

-Who killed Lorraine and why?

-You don't listen too good, do you? Keep out of it.

-Did you kill my sister?

-No. I didn't.

-But, you know who killed her.

It was not a question, but Mr Dana answered it.

-So do you.

-What are you telling me? I don't know who killed Lorraine. At least tell me why she was murdered.

-Read this morning's papers.

-Why should I.

-Maybe, you shouldn't. Anyway, I've said too much. Just keep your trap shut and you might make it to your next birthday.

-Get the hell out of here! And, thanks for nothing.

Mr. Dana made for the door. He held it open.

-Like it or not, baby, you're involved. Just stay on the outer perimeter of things. Think you can do that?

-Get out!

The door clicked shut as April threw her slipper at it. Quickly, she got dressed and went down to the newspaper stand to pick up a copy of the morning news. She'd forgotten all about her hangover.

April sat at the counter of Chock full o' Nuts sipping her black coffee with no sugar. It took that waitress long enough to bring it over. She scanned through the Daily Mirror, her favorite paper. It covered the metro news thoroughly and with an almost intimate touch. She read every headline and even the advertisements. Nothing so far. Had she missed something obvious? She turned to the Sports Section. Nothing. Entertainment Section that even covered television. Still nothing.

There was only one thing left to do: go through it again and order another cup of coffee.

-Oh, waitress?

-I'll be right with you, Miss.

-Coffee black, no sugar.

-Just give me a minute, please.

-Sure.

Bitch.

April started with the front page headlines again. Go with the most obvious, always. It didn't take her too long to spot a familiar face and therefore she even read the first and last paragraphs. "Mayhem at the Museum." She spotted Edward Mendez's name.

"Last night at the Museum of Natural History pandemonium broke out at the private exhibition of the Sumerian artifacts that had recently been brought in by person or persons not yet identified. A Mr. Werner Hoffman was taken to Roosevelt Hospital after allegedly coming into contact with a particular artifact that purportedly gave off a near fatal sound...some sort of vibration which drove most spectators from the exhibit hall. Mr. Hoffman is said to have suffered irreparable brain damage and there is little hope for a recovery.

"Edward Mendez, P. I. was at the scene and it was the detective who managed to dislodge the Sumerian urn from Mr. Hoffman's grasp – the latter seeming not to be able to let go of the object.

"The urn, if that is what it actually is, has not been recovered. The police are investigating the theft and the urn's origin. The exhibit hall has been temporarily closed off to visitors until further notice."

April placed the paper on to the counter and folded it over. She was more puzzled than ever. What did any of this have to do with her and sister, Lorraine? Nothing...but it must mean something or why did that man who called himself Jack Dana tell her to read the papers? And, where was that waitress with her coffee?

-Your coffee, Miss.

-Thanks. It took you long enough.

-Sorry. Is that your paper?

-Yes.

-You finished with it?

-No.

This waitress had built-in gall.

-Anything else?

-No.

Another customer sat down and got the waitress' attention.

-I have to talk to Mr. Mendez. I'll call him.

April glanced at her wristwatch. She had to catch the train for work. She'd probably have to work overtime to make up for this morning's absence. She finished her coffee and left the exact change on the counter with no T.I.P..

April was sitting at her desk. She had just finished typing a series of "rejection" letters to various would-be authors. Her boss, a senior editor, had to sign them so she brought them into his office.

-Okay, April, that's it for now. Why don't you take a coffee break? You don't mind staying a little late to-night, do you?

-Not really. But, I will take that coffee break. Want me to bring you back a cup?

-No, thanks. I'm cutting back.

April went downstairs to her friend who worked in the Publicity Dept. Coffee was the last thing on her mind.

-Hey, Margo? Mind if I use your phone for a few minutes?

-Help yourself, hon'. Or better yet, go in my boss' office for some privacy. He's not coming in today.

-Thanks.

April went into the small office, closed the door be-hind her and dialed Edward Mendez's number.

-Edward Mendez's office.

-Mr. Mendez, please. It's April Keyes and I've gotta' speak to him.

-Right away, Miss Keyes.

The P. I. got on the line.

-April? Where you calling from?

-Thank God you're there, Mr. Mendez. I'm calling from work. I've gotta' tell you what happened to me this morning.

-Shoot.

April related everything that had happened that morning, including the newspaper article.

-Mr. Mendez, what does that article about some relic have to do with my sister's murder?

-This Jack Dana – which is probably an alias – might just want to confuse you and put a good scare into you.

-He hit the bulls eye...twice.

-April what do you know about your sister's personal life?

-Come to think of it, not all that much. I was a lot more talkative than she was. She was a good listener, sort of on the quiet side, at least with me.

-Listen. Don't come to my office. Call me from an outside line.

-Okay.

-They're probably watching you, but don't let it worry you.

-Oh, please don't say that.

-I had to for your own sake. Go about your daily routine and keep me posted if anything else happens. I'll do the detective work. Savvy?

-That's just fine by me. And, I better get back to my desk.

-And, April? Play it real cool. And, call me Edward.

A clue, Jack Dana or whoever he was, had deliberately thrown the linking clue into Edward Mendez's lap.

The Sumerian urn had to be somehow linked to Lorraine Keyes. And, now, where to begin?

Edward thought good and hard about that. And, the answer came to him rather quickly. He had to grill Marlena and demand the entire truth from the woman.

He called ahead to make sure that she was home.

-Of course, dear boy, come right over.

Edward arrived at the townhouse in twenty minutes. And Marlena had some alarming news of her own for the P. I. Werner Hoffman had escaped from his confinement at Roosevelt Hospital after having assaulted and cannibalized two interns.

Edward sat down in the nearest armchair. He tried to comprehend and make some sort of sense from what he had just heard.

-But, the man is less that a damned vegetable. Dr. Ingram was positive about that.

Marlena sat down in the opposite armchair.

-A misdiagnosis, obviously. He can walk and attack with no compunction to killing.

-A ruthless killing machine? Have the police put a dragnet out for him? They must've by this time if I know Lt. Donovan.

-An APB was put out. He shouldn't be too difficult to spot.

Edward reached for a cigarette. The hell with the bubble gum for now. He lit up and took a deep drag.

-I wonder...maybe some of his brain repaired itself or wasn't as seriously damaged as Dr. Ingram thought.

No. That chick is too good at her job. And, where is he headed for? He escaped to go where and do what?

-Good questions, Edward. Can you put forward a P. I. theory?

Edward took another drag on his cigarette.

-Maybe...just maybe...he's looking for the urn. And, it couldn't have been Hoffman who Susan and I spotted last night lurking about.

He answered his own query.

-Just about impossible. I'd just left him in restraints at the hospital. So, what the hell can he be up to?

Marlena looked Edward straight in the eye.

-I've no idea.

April Keyes walked the short distance to her apartment from the elevated train station. It was getting dark, but twilight lingered in the sky. She entered her apartment building and was about to climb the stairwell to her apartment when a man grabbed her from behind. He placed one hand over her mouth and with the other, he pinned her arms behind her back.

-Don't struggle. You won't break free.

She stopped struggling.

-Good. You do what you're told, sometimes. Now, listen real good. You contacted that private dick. Mistake. You get just one more chance, Miss Keyes. Leave town. Pack your bags tonight and grab the first and fastest train headed west. You're getting a break and that doesn't happen too often. Take it and don't look it in the face. Now...talk.

-I just can't pack up and leave.

-You can and you will. They'll kill you otherwise.

-But, I don't know anything.

-You might know more than you think. Your sister was in it up to her neck.

-Into what? What are you talking about?

-Leave town, Miss Keyes. Leave town early tomorrow morning. Try Vegas. That town's about to explode. Pretty girl like you should make out good. Why not take a plane out there? Just a friendly suggestion.

-Please, you're hurting me.

-They'll kill you...or-

-What?

-I'm doing you a favor. Things might get ugly in the city real soon. Things might get real dangerous for you.

-Oh, God!

-It's up to you.

He let April go and left by the front door.

EIGHT

IT WAS early morning and the sun was just about to rise. It was going to be a cool and breezy day and Edward was no closer to solving the murder of Lorraine Keyes.

Who had known the girl? Not her sister, April. They hadn't shared secrets...maybe. Should he pay another visit to Tom Cooper? Could April possibly be with him? And, that urn of Marlena's and Werner Hoffman's disappearance...were they all linked somehow?

The P. I. had two leads- no, three leads: Tom Cooper, Marlena and the foundling home. He picked Tom Cooper and if he wasn't up, he'd wake the bastard up and put the fear of God in him...that is, after he paid April Keyes a personal visit.

-You got me, Mister. Just up and left. Not so much as a farewell note.

Edward Mendez had taken a good look around April Keyes' apartment: clothes, toiletries and jewelry were all gone as far as the P. I. could tell. He turned around to face the landlady.

-You heard her come in last night.

It wasn't a question.

-I sure did. She likes wearing those high heels of hers. She's got the legs for them. I'll give her that.

-And, she never mentioned any place that she'd like to visit, did she?

-Frisco. She said that she might like to move out there. Never seen the Pacific Ocean. Me neither, for that matter.

-Thanks, Mrs.-

-Simmons. Rosalie Simmons.

-If Miss Keyes should drop you a line, let me know, will you?

Edward handed the woman his business card.

-Mr. Mendez? Is she in any kind of trouble with the law. These young girls today are wild.

-No, Mrs. Simmons. But, she *could* be in trouble.

-She's running scared; that's it, isn't it?

-Mrs. Simmons, you oughta' be a detective.

Edward's next stop was to that suburb in Jersey City. The trip to Jersey was fast, there was no traffic and Edward already had the lay of the land. He pulled up to Tom Cooper's traditional 1920's home and rang the front doorbell. Once again, the door was answered almost immediately.

-Mr. Mendez? You here, again?

-Mind if I come in?

-I guess not.

Tom Cooper stepped aside and let the P. I. in.

-Tommy, where is Gordon Prentiss? Give, man.

-You don't footsy around, do you. I already told you. I don't know.

-Sure you do.

-I don't. After my parents were killed he and the girls went back to that foundling home where they came from. I never saw him again.

-What were your parents like?

-I'm not too sure how to answer that.

-Were they good to you?

-Of course.

-Were they average folk?

-What does this have to do with anything?

-Maybe nothing.

-Mr. Mendez, I've got nothing else to tell you.

-Did I see you opening up window shutters as I drove in?

-What of it? I close up tight for the night. Always did. Always.

-You're sweating, Tom.

-I don't like your questions.

-Are you afraid at night, Tommy? Is that the reason for the closed shutters?

Edward's P. I. gut instinct was kicking in. This boy was scared, but of what or whom?

-You can tell me.

-All right. Yeah. And, if you knew of what, you'd be plenty scared, too.

-Of what...of whom?

Tom Cooper smiled slyly.

-Of both. Are you ready to leave now, 'cause I've got things to do?

The P. I. went over to the Precinct House which was handling the Lorraine Keyes murder case. Detective Hopper was at his desk, chain smoking.

-Hello, Ed Mendez. Take a load off.

Edward sat down, took out a cigarette and lit up.

-I hear you've been nosing around the Lorraine Keyes murder.

-You heard right.

-Anything new on it?

Edward gave all the pertinent information to the detective.

-So, you think this Gordon Prentiss, who did a vanishing act, might be the girl's killer?

-It did flicker across my mind, but-

-Motive?

-Motive. Why kill the girl in broad daylight?

The P. I. answered his own question.

-I think that she and I were being followed and ...the murder was on the spur of the moment because she'd been talking to yours truly.

Detective Hopper leaned back in his chair and smiled.

-Little secrets whispered between the sheets. By the way, was she any good?

Now, it was Edward's turn to smile.

-After a couple of more rounds, maybe.

-So, why'd they jump the gun?

-Assassins don't take chances.

-Assassins?

-This was a professional hit. I reeks of it.

-I'll buy that. But, why, for Christ's sake?

Edward let out a puff of smoke.

-Beats me. And, that's why I'm here.

-Keep talking to me, pal.

-Could I take a look at the contents of Lorraine's purse, again? Maybe, I missed something.

-Sure. Just stay put, and I'll get it for you.

Detective Hopper was back in under two minutes. He handed Edward what looked like a very high-end shoulder bag: black patent leather with a long, gold mesh chain. He opened it up.

-Hmm. Nice scent. My former girlfriend would know what brand it is.

-Smells kind of expensive, like fifty bucks an ounce.

-Let's see what we've got here...lipstick, compact...those keys that you showed me the other day. Let's have a look at her wallet. This chick had a wad of money on her.

-Two hundred bucks if I remember right. A lot of change to be carrying around.

-Yep. And a library card. That might tell us something. Mind if I take this with me, Detective?

-Be my guest, but keep me posted. Plan on checking out a few libraries?

-I'll start in her own neighborhood and work my way uptown.

-Good luck, Mendez. And, I'll keep you posted.

-Thanks.

Edward not only hit the jackpot in his first library visit, but he just happened upon an old acquaintance of his.

-Henriette Miller. You're just about the last person I expected to see. Are you a librarian here?

-I am. I have given up my pre-med studies and graduated with a degree in Ancient History.

-Well, good for you.

-And, how may I help you, Mr. Private Detective?

-I need to know if a Lorraine Keyes ever took out any books from this library branch.

-I will check for you, Edward. It's easy enough.

Henriette went to the "lending" files. And, Edward felt awkward about his next question.

-Where have you been keeping yourself? You just dropped out of sight.

-Ah! Here it is. And, to answer your tactful question: Lt. Donovan and I drifted apart. There was no rancor.

-I guess it's really none of my business.

-I wouldn't say that. You are his friend and you were curious. I don't mind. Now, lets see what Miss Keyes likes to read.

Edward and Henriette scanned down the list. Henriette was puzzled. Edward let out a long, low whistle. Miss Miller was the first to speak.

-But, these are very technical books. Was Miss Keyes a scientist?

-I'd say, no.

-Perhaps, she took them out for a friend.

-I think you've got something there, Henriette. Would any of these books still be on the shelves?

-Why don't we check and see? It won't take long. These books are all from the same section.

-Lead on.

Within a few minutes, Edward and Henriette were sitting at one of the reading tables leafing through the technical books that Lorraine Keyes had taken out. The P. I. grinned to himself just reading the titles: "Sound, Vibration and Pressure," "Velocity and the Speed of Sound," "Breaking the Sound Barrier" and "Weaponry and Sound."

-My God. If Lorraine didn't read these then who on Earth did?

-A boyfriend, perhaps?

-Maybe. Or maybe the man who killed her.

Henriette was leafing through the "Weaponry and Sound" book.

-Edward, there are notations and under-linings. Fortunately, they are in pencil and can be erased.

-Not on your life, Henriette. I'm gonna' be borrowing these books myself.

-What was Miss Keyes line of work?

-Interior Design or so she said.

-Perhaps, she was looking into recording apparatus and how they would filter through the walls of houses or apartments.

-That's one big, long shot, but an interesting one. But...I'm not buying it.

-But, how does this connect with her murder?

-You got me, but somehow it does...it has to.

Henriette sat back for a moment before asking her next question.

-I read a story once in one of those metaphysical magazines about the nature of God.

-What about Him?

-That God and creation, itself, is pressure maintained by the human mind.

-You know, Henriette, when you said "metaphysical," I was reminded of that Sumerian exhibit that I went to the other night.

-Yes! I read about that and what happened. I wish I had been there. But, how dreadful for Mr. Hoffman. Edward, was it sound...pressure...that caused it?

-Oh, man. The connection, Henriette, that's the connection: sound and vibration...vibration that's deafening, but more than just deafening.

Henriette tapped her pencil on the spine of one of the books.

-Edward, did you know that in the Bible, the walls of Jericho came tumbling down because of sound?

-Marlena Lake mentioned that once; a weapon she called it. A weapon that was even more destructive than an Atomic Bomb...sound that could shatter even steel and concrete.

-It's almost frightening to even think of it. The technology was lost and I suppose that we should be grateful for that.

Edward got up from his chair.

-Henriette, I've gotta' take these books with me, but I haven't got a library card.

-I have. I'll take them out for you. Will you promise to keep me apprised of your progress? And, I would love to meet this fascinating Marlena Lake some day.

-I got a feeling that your wish is gonna' come true.

And, then, a silence descended upon the two people...an unexpected silence.

-Henriette?

-Yes. I feel it, too. A silence that one feels.

-Like the deadly calm before the fatal storm.

-A girlfriend of mine had moved to Carson City, Nevada. She was traveling just outside the city limits in her car and she felt that terrible stillness.

-What happened?

-An earthquake hit. It wasn't severe, but it did cause some minor damage to property. And, when the earthquake came, it was almost a relief from that silence that had pervaded the air.

The P. I. nodded and took out a cigarette, but didn't light up.

-You know something, Henriette? It's as if that stillness has been with me ever since I started out on this case.

NINE

APRIL KEYES had a window seat on the plane heading out to Las Vegas. It was late afternoon and the sunlight came streaming in through the windows on April's side of the small passenger plane. The young girl gazed out the window at the blue sky and the desert below. She wasn't afraid of this new adventure even though she was fleeing for her life. She'd never been this far west. And, the fact that she didn't have any prospects in this strange city was kind of exhilarating...even exciting.

April had deposited her sister's insurance check into her own bank account: $25,000. My goodness. What a windfall! How had Lorraine managed the monthly payments? That sum of money along with her own savings gave her a reasonable "safety" net. She could take her time finding the right job and a decent apartment. She wouldn't have to just settle on some dump.

April was wearing one of Lorraine's black dresses. It was an expensive designer cut and it felt just great wearing it. She had taken several of her sister's dresses. They were the same size, after all, and why shouldn't she be wearing them? How much had this entire ensemble cost her sister? What had her sister, Lorraine, done to afford all this?

The young girl was about to close her eyes for a few moments when someone sat down next to her. It was a woman: a beautiful and carefully made-up woman. Her blonde hair was up-swept and lacquered into place and she was wearing diamond earrings and a necklace to match. Her beige dress was simply cut and she had on stiletto heels.

-I spotted you, hon', when we were boarding. My name's Ada Lamont.

-Oh. April Keyes. Nice meeting you.

-I just love your dress. I'll bet it's straight from Paris.

-It was my sister's. I don't know where she bought it. But, thanks for the compliment.

-From Paris. Take my word for it. Is this your first trip to Vegas, April? I can always tell.

-It's my first real trip out west. I'm kind of excited and scared...but more excited.

-Scared? Don't be. A pretty girl like you will make out great. Take my word for it. Any prospects?

-Not a one. This trip was sort of spur of the moment.

-Then this is your lucky day. I'm a showgirl over at the Ritz Casino. I've got connections in this town...big connections. And, my boyfriend just happens to be the owner and manager of Diamond Dice. His name's Tony Montana. Isn't that a kick?

April wasn't sure how to react to all this. Ada continued.

-I'll introduce you to him. He'll find you a spot in no time. And, don't you go making eyes at him, either.

April laughed.

-I won't. I just hope I won't be too scared to speak. I'm kind of shy around strangers.

-He's a charmer. Let him do the talking.

The plane started to descend.

-Where you putting up for the night? At the Sands? It's kind of expensive.

-Oh, gosh. I don't know. I thought maybe the cab driver could recommend something.

-Ada, here, can recommend something for you. I've got a house just a couple of miles off Freemont, that's where most of the action is. You can camp out with me 'til you get your own digs.

-Are you sure, Ada? I don't want to put you out.

-So, who's being put out? I got a spare bedroom and there's plenty of food in the 'frig.. I've even got an overhead fan.

The plane hit the airstrip and taxied over toward the airport terminal.

-Okay, April, get your stuff and we'll head on over to the parking lot. My car's over there...or it should be.

April noticed the subtle change in Ada's demeanor. The two women claimed their luggage and made their way over to the airport parking lot.

-There it is.

Ada waved to the man sitting behind the steering wheel of a blue and white Chevrolet. April was starting to feel a little uneasy about this instant "friendship" with a complete stranger.

-Maybe, I shouldn't.

-Shouldn't what, hon'? It's Tony and he's harmless most of the time.

There was another man in the back seat of the car. He got out and opened the trunk while keeping his back to the two women. They walked over to where he was standing and handed him their luggage. He slammed the trunk closed, still keeping his back to them, and once more got into the back seat.

-I'm gonna' sit up front with Tony. You get in back with Mr. Gruesome.

April was about halfway in when the man seized her and put a cotton cloth over her mouth...a cotton cloth laced with chloroform.

-What's going on back there? What are you doing to that girl?

-She fainted. It must be the desert heat.

-It better be the heat. You didn't do anything to her, did you?

-Just turn around and mind your own damned business.

Ada turned to Tony who was looking straight ahead at the road.

-Tony, you said no one was gonna' get hurt. And, are you gonna' let him talk to me like that?

-She fainted, Ada. Just leave it at that.

-Whee are we headed?

-To the house. She can sleep it off there.

In another twenty minutes, they turned off the main road and on to a side street in a newly built residential area. Tony parked the car in front of the one story house. There was no lawn or fence. The grounds around each house were bare. Tony handed Ada the keys to the front door.

-Get out and open the place up. And, don't look back.

Ada knew not to argue with that tone of voice from Tony. She did as she was told.

April was removed from the car and carried into the house. Ada turned on the lights.

-Put her in the bedroom. Ada, make her comfortable and come right out.

-Sure. Sure, Tony. Anything you say.

Ada closed the bedroom door behind her. She took off April's shoes and tried to revive her.

-Honey, can you hear me?

April stirred. She was semi-conscious and knew that she was in danger.

-Are you awake? It's Ada.

April tried to speak.

-Call him up, please.

-Call who up? Who do you want me to call?

-Edward...

-Honey, give me a last name. There must be a million Edwards in the phone book.

-Edward Mendez. He'll help. He's in New York.

April slipped back into unconsciousness.

There was a banging on the door.

-Hey, Ada, what's goin' on in there?

-I'm coming out.

Tony came in.

-She under?

-She's under, all right. You're not gonna' hurt her, are you? She's just a kid.

-Kids are nothing but trouble. Let's go. Jack's gonna' handle this.

-Handle what?

-You're too damned nosy for your own good. Now, shut up! We're leaving. And, just remember: you've never seen this place or that chick on the bed.

Ada's survival instinct kicked in.

-Whatever you say, Tony. Whatever you say.

-Let's get out of here.

-Okay, Tony, level with me. What's this all about? Who is that girl?

-April Keyes.

-I know that. Why all the drama?

-The chick's a liability to persons you're better off not knowing. Light me a cigarette, will you?

-Sure. She's as good as dead, isn't she?

-Beats me.

Ada looked out on to the vast desert landscape: a perfect grave site for a corpse that's never meant to be found. She turned back to Tony.

-Who was that guy? Never seen him before. Friend of yours? He gives me the creeps.

Tony smiled.

-Nope. Jack is nobody's friend.

-An executioner, huh?

Tony turned the car on to Fremont St.

TEN

EDWARD WAS greeted at the door by Irene Wong. She looked distressed and puzzled.

-Edward, I'm so glad you've come. Marlena is in a state and not even Susan can calm her down. Maybe, you can.

Edward was shown into the living room.

-She's in the library with Susan. I'm sure it's all right if you go right in.

-Thanks. You joining me, Irene?

-No. Not this time. I'll be in my room with my notes.

Edward walked on into the library. He could hear Marlena's raised voice.

-Marlena?

-Edward, dear boy. Come in and shut the door behind you.

Susan was sitting down and looking in Edward's direction. It was hard to tell what she was thinking.

-What's up, Marlena?

-Have a seat, please. I've much to tell you.

Edward sat opposite Susan while Marlena paced the floor between them.

-It's simply incredible. It's an outrage! They simply come in here and help themselves to my property...my property!

Susan dared to speak.

-The Sumerian urn, Edward. The police confiscated it.

-I'll call my attorneys. I'll sue the city...the mayor!

Edward crossed his legs and let Marlena blow off more steam.

-A priceless piece of antiquity...stolen by the Manhattan police force. It's...it's unforgivable. I won't stand for it!

Susan was going to correct her mother, but thought better of it. Edward didn't.

-Marlena, which Precinct was it?

She turned on him.

-Can't you guess? Who else would it be? That rotten, condescending bastard, Lt. Donovan. I'll have him thrown off the Force.

-I'm sure that Lt. Donovan was just doing his job, Marlena. They're probably holding it as evidence. They *will* give it back to you, unless-

Marlena stopped her pacing and stood directly in front of the P. I.

-Go on, Edward.

-Unless it's too dangerous to handle...a threat to the general public. The police have to take that as a priority.

-Their *having* it is a threat to the general public. Edward, as I'm certain that you have surmised that urn is a weapon...a weapon from the depths of antiquity. It predates any known record of mankind. It's value is inconceivable, no price could be placed on it.

-Don't be too sure about that. But, Marlena, now that I think about it, what's the word on Werner Hoffman? Has he been caught?

-How would I know? Ask Lt. Donovan or one of his minions. Who cares about a vegetable?

-When I leave here, I will.

Susan leaned forward in her chair.

-He must have been caught by now. He has no mind left. It's a miracle that he can function at all.

Edward took out a cigarette.

-I don't know about that. Something or some instinct drove him on.

-Drove him on to *what*?

-A purpose.

Susan couldn't accept this and said so.

-The man's brain is a mass of jelly. How could he even walk about or even balance himself?

-It's supposed to be impossible for a bumble bee to fly, but somehow they do it. They must possess some kind of physical strength or an unknown aerodynamic mechanism that we don't know about. And, maybe, our consciousness doesn't come from our brain after all. Maybe, it's hovering right outside our bodies. Who knows?

Marlena broke in.

-Edward is right. The damned bee does fly. And, all philosophy aside, I believe that Werner Hoffman is looking for the urn. He's being *drawn* to it somehow.

Edward thought that Marlena's theory was plausible if somewhat inexplicable.

-Maybe. But, where is he? If he hasn't been caught, then where is he hiding?

-Who cares? Forget about Werner Hoffman for now. I must have that urn back. The police may ship it off to some God forsaken laboratory. It could be damaged or-

-Or what, Marlena? Give. You know more about that urn than you're telling.

Marlena sat down.

-Edward? Have you read your Bible as I've advised you to?

-As a matter of fact, yes.

-Good. How did the walls of Jericho come tumbling down?

-It was sound...vibration that cracked the walls. I just had a brief history lesson from a very learned librarian.

-Yes. And, that urn can do similar damage.

-Keep going. What else can it do?

-I believe that it can raise the dead.

-Now, you're putting me on.

-No I'm not, Edward. Lazarus was raised from the dead. It can be done. It *has* been done.

Nathalie Montaigne was sitting on the sofa in her second floor apartment above her book store. A paperback novel was on her lap that she had wanted to read. She had not even turned the first page. Werner Hoffman was on her mind and more specifically, his assets.

Nathalie was a practical woman of the world. She must look after her own interests...her own survival and, of course, comfort. Her business partner was brain dead or so she had been told. And, why shouldn't she believe those physicians? Surely, they knew their business and could recognize when a man is as good as dead if not better off dead. Tomorrow, she would go to her attorney and take over the business at hand and appoint herself executor of her dead partner's estate. It should be quite simple: she was his beneficiary and not his son who currently resided in Germany. His son who she would keep ignorant of his father's pathetic condition. She would spare him the trauma of knowing. Why burden the poor boy?

But, was Werner attempting to steal the urn at the exhibit? How very foolish of him if that were the case. He would have never gotten away with it.

She noticed the novel on her lap. She put it aside and stood up. The downstairs buzzer was ringing. Who could it be? She knew very few people and callers to her home were rare. The buzzer kept ringing.

-I will go down and see who it is.

She descended the one flight of stairs and looked through the peephole. She did not recognize the man who was standing there.

-But, who is calling, please?

-You do not know me; but, I know of you.

-Indeed. So, who are you?

-I am Manuel Mendez.

Nathalie recognized the name immediately. She had to catch her breath. This evening might not be so boring after all.

-Please, do come in. I am alone and that is the reason for my hesitation.

-I understand. My manservant will wait in the car.

Nathalie led Manuel Mendez upstairs and in to her apartment where she offered him the comfort of her favorite armchair.

-May I offer you a drink?

-No. Thank you. I haven't much time and neither have you.

-What do you mean by that, Mr. Mendez? Am I in some sort of danger? I will tell you that danger is not unknown to me.

-The danger that I speak of is abhorrent even to me. I will get straight to the point. That Sumerian urn must be retrieved, if that is possible.

-Tell me why. You must.

-Your former partner knew of its power. The fool fell into the trap of arrogance. He is now wandering the streets looking for...

-For what? Tell me.

-No. For whom.

-Who does he look for?

-For you, Miss Montaigne.

-Mon Dieu! But, he is brain dead, no?

-Yes. But, certain facets still operate in a perverted form. You would do well to lock your door and windows.

-You frighten me. Is it safe for me to stay here?

-No. You may be my house guest until Mr. Hoffman is caught or drops dead of his own accord.

-And, what of the urn? What can I possibly do about that?

-Pack a suitcase, Miss Montaigne. We must get you to safety first.

-But, you haven't answered my question.

-You will assist me in my efforts to get it back.

ELEVEN

ADA LAMONT was a showgirl. Period. She had no further ambitions in life beyond that. It's not that she was lazy or unintelligent. She was practical and had no illusions about herself and her limited talents. And, she was happy with her job. She was good at it. She was a crowd pleaser and very pretty...bordering on beautiful with a lovely and voluptuous figure. The fact that she was pushing thirty was shoved into the back of her mind. If she took care of herself and kept her figure, she'd have five more profitable years in Vegas.

But, tonight, she was tired and just a little worried. And, worried about some little girl who she barely knew. A kid. A pretty kid who must be in deep trouble up to her pretty little neck.Why should Ada care one fig about her? Maybe because she was part of the set-up? The whole thing bothered her. And, what was that name that the girl whispered to her? Edward Mendez, the detective. Ada remembered his name from the papers. Should she call the private dick? No. Oh, no! It would have to be a long distance call and...no. Not from the hotel. It would be on their records sheet. From a phone booth...maybe. And, maybe it was already too late. If the girl was in danger, they wouldn't keep her alive for too long.

No. Look out for yourself. Keep to your own business. A long distance phone call was too big of a gamble. She'd be spotted. Tony would find out. She couldn't take the risk. After all, he was her meal ticket.

Tony walked in.

-You still up, babe?

-Just getting ready to turn in.

-You look kinda' worried. Why don't you tell Tony all about it.

-Nothing to tell.

Tony took off his tie.

-Don't lie to me. You're no good at it.

-I'm not lying to you.

-Let's get to it: don't even think of helping that girl.

-I wasn't. I'm no sap.

-Good. Stick to the runway. You'll live a lot longer.

-What the hell does that mean?

-It means shut your trap. Now, what did that girl tell you?

-I already told you: nothing.

-Liar.

Tony moved closer to Ada. He was still holding on to his tie. He backed Ada into a corner.

-Don't call me that, Tony.

-What did she tell you? Give or this tie goes around your neck.

-Nothing. I swear. She was out like a light.

-Give!

Ada could smell Tony's breath. It was laced with Scotch.

-Tony-

He pressed her hard against the wall. She could feel his erection.

-Feel that, baby. I get excited when I push it in or kill someone. What's it gonna' be? Huh? Huh?

Ada was scared...really scared. She had to tell what she knew. Her life was on the line.

-Edward Mendez. I think she wanted me to call him.

-Mendez? The private dick in New York? Well, you ain't calling no one. If I catch you even looking at a phone, I'll cut your tongue out.

-Tony, please. I wouldn't. I swear.

-Good. That's real good.

Tony backed off.

-Now, babe, let's get to bed. Look at me. I'm still hard for you.

Henriette Miller was in a happy mood while on her way home. Maybe...just maybe...a little too happy. The young, German girl didn't have many friends and seeing Edward Mendez today was such an unexpected pleasure. Such an interesting man and so handsome and charming. Truth be told, she missed hearing from Lt. Donovan. The Lieutenant was also an interesting man if just a bit older than she. Still, he was educated and nice in a sort of gruff way.

Henriette was walking along Highland Place toward Highland Park. It was a brisk, Autumn evening with a full moon hovering in the sky. She looked up at the moon and felt her mood change to a sense of dread verging on fear. She quickened her pace. Were those the sounds of footsteps coming up from behind her? She wanted to scream. She didn't. Instead, she started to run towards her apartment building. It was just ahead on the corner facing the park.

As Henriette started to run, she opened her purse and took out her house keys. Was she putting distance between herself and those footsteps? Yes! She ran faster, reached the outer door to her apartment building, unlocked the door and slammed it shut behind her.

Henriette ran up the foyer stairs. She unlocked that door and slammed that door shut. Now, she ran to her apartment which was right off the hallway on the first floor. She undid both locks. And, as soon as she was in her apartment, she put the safety chain on in addition to the two locks.

Now that she could breathe a little easier, Henriette's curiosity got the best of her. Quickly, and as silently as she could, she went to the kitchen window and peeked through the Venetian blinds. She wanted to see who had been chasing her.

The street lamp illuminated the sidewalk giving her a closer view of any passerby. She waited. No one came. Had he turned about and gone in the opposite direction? There! He was coming into view. It was a man. He was wearing an ill fitting suit. Were those blood stains on his suit? Yes. Henriette had been a nursing student and knew the sight of blood when she saw it. For the moment, this drew her attention away from the man's face.

The face was a white mask...a death mask. If this man had once been handsome, that was forever buried in the past. His arms hung limp at his sides as he shuffled along the pavement looking from left to right. Henriette drew back from the window. Had he seen her? Had eye contact been made? The man moved forward and crossed the street. He was going into the park...the park that abutted on to the cemetery.

Ada Lamont got up and out of bed. She couldn't sleep and she needed to sleep. She slipped on her robe and went into the living room. Tony was still asleep. She walked over to the sliding glass door that let out to the balcony. Maybe the cold, desert air would calm her because something had to. But, only one thing would do it. She stopped short of opening the sliding door and walked over to the phone on the end table by the sofa. And, this time, she didn't hesitate.

-Hello, operator? Put me through to Edward Mendez in New York City. Manhattan. And, please, hurry.

Ada looked at the clock on the mantle. It read 5 A.M. Damn it! Too early. It's only 8 A.M. In New York. He might not be in. And, what the hell is taking that operator so long?

-I'm putting your call through, Madame.

-Thanks.

About time, too.

The phone rang, but there was no answer.

-I knew it was too early.

And, then, Edward's answering service came on.

-Edward Mendez's line. May I help you?

-Mr. Mendez, please.

-This is Mr. Mendez's answering service.

-Can you reach him for me? It's urgent.

-If it is urgent, I can try his home number.

-Then, try it and hurry.

Ada was struggling to keep her voice calm. The last thing she wanted to do was sound like an hysterical woman which she was close to becoming.

-Operator...just keep ringing. Someone's gotta' pick up.

-I am, Madame, but there seems to be no one picking up. One moment, please.

-Hello? Who is calling?

-Is this Mr. Mendez's line?

-It's his home. Who is calling?

-You don't know me, but I've gotta' speak to Mr. Mendez.

-I'm afraid he's not at home at the moment.

-Then, who am I talking to?

-Nella Mendez.

-His wife?

-His sister.

-My name's Ada Lamont. Listen, Miss Mendez, I've gotta hang up in a minute. Tell Mr. Mendez that April Keyes is in Vegas. She's in trouble and it might be too late as it is. I know. I should have called sooner. But-

Tony grabbed the receiver out of Ada's hand and slammed it down.

-You idiot! You prized little idiot. Do you know what you've done?

Ada backed away.

-Tony, I never mentioned your name.

-You mentioned his name and your name which is just as damned good.

He kept pointing his finger at her, maneuvering her toward the balcony...forcing her against the sliding door.

-Just as good as a signed confession. Slide open that door you double-crossing bitch! Open it up. Now!

Ada slid open the door and practically stumbled on to the balcony. She caught a hold of the iron railing and steadied herself.

-You're goin' places, baby, like straight down ten stories.

Tony made to grab Ada, but just then an Atomic Bomb blast was set off in the desert. The flash and burst of sound took Tony by surprise. Ada, who was street tough, caught Tony off guard and as he came at her, she tripped him up. He hit the railing with his groin and leaned dangerously forward. Ada finished him off. She shoved him over. Tony went plummeting down to his death. His screams stopped when his body hit the pavement.

Ada Lamont had to think fast and that meant think survival. She leaned over the balcony railing. People were already gathering around what had been Tony Montana. A few of them were looking up. Ada pulled away from the railing. More people would be coming out to get a look at the gruesome sight, but that didn't bother the seasoned call girl. The police wouldn't be too far away and hotel management might already be on their way up.

She went to the coffee table and got herself a cigarette. Easy girl...you can get out of this. Ada sat down on the edge of the sofa. She put out the cigarette and picked up the phone.

-Hello, Rex? It's Ada. My God, Tony just took a header off the balcony.

-Is that what's going on out there?

-Rex, please, get up here. We were waiting for the A-bomb test. And, I guess the flash caught Tony off guard. He was leaning too far over the railing.

-Ada, I'll be right up. Keep cool and don't talk to anyone until I get there. You listening?

-I won't let anyone in until you get here, Rex. And, thanks.

He hung up the phone.

Well done, Ada. Rex was a friend; a professional gambler in his own right with ties to the Vegas mob. He liked Ada. He and Tony had gotten along, but were never really friends.

Now, she could have that cigarette.

TWELVE

EDWARD MENDEZ spent the night at Marlena's townhouse. He'd gone to bed with more questions raised than had been answered...a lot more questions. He almost smiled to himself. Lorraine Keyes' murder was linked to Gordon Prentiss and Tom Cooper. One or both men had had a hand in it. But, where in hell was Gordon Prentiss? You don't just drop off the face of the Earth. The guy must have taken on a new identity. And, he had every right to do just that, but it doesn't change the birth certificate if there ever was one.

The P. I. had two calls on his schedule tomorrow: a visit to Miss Matthews out in New Jersey at the foundling home and a visit to Ginny Gray to see what progress she had made.

Edward couldn't sleep. It was past dawn so why not check with his answering service. There was a phone in his room.

-Hello. Edward Mendez here. Any messages for me?

-There was a long distance call from Las Vegas, Mr. Mendez. It was forwarded to your home number.

-From whom?

-A Miss Ada Lamont.

-Who?

-Miss Lamont.

-Was the call picked up?

-I believe that it was.

-Thank you.

Edward dialed his mother's phone number. Nella picked up.

First things first: Ada Lamont's phone call had told Edward where April Keyes had fled to: Las Vegas, Nevada. The girl was probably dead; no reason to keep her alive and every reason to kill her. Chances are the body would never be found. A loose end that was sort of tied up. Foolish girl. Her safest bet had been to stay put in New York. Edward could have gotten her protection.

Edward pulled up in front of the foundling home, lit himself a cigarette and went on in.

He was greeted by a rather severe looking woman with a very short and severe haircut. She sat erect and looked him straight in the eye.

-May I help you?

-Miss Matthews?

-I am she.

-Edward Mendez. We spoke on the phone the other day.

-Yes. I remember our conversation.

-I'll get straight to the point. Where is Gordon Prentiss, Miss Matthews? It's a matter of life and death.

Miss Matthews took a deep breath before answering the P. I.

-Please, sit down, Mr. Mendez.

-Thank you.

Edward sat down and tapped some cigarette ash into the ashtray on Miss Matthews' desk. He could see that she was a smoker like himself.

-Give, Miss Mathews. And, please don't play fancy with me. A young girl has already been killed.

-I don't honestly know where Gordon Prentiss is.

-I said don't play fancy with me. So, what's his new identity, huh? And, where is this "new" person hiding? And, I'm not joking. If you're holding out on me, I'll have you sent up for withholding information regarding a felon.

Miss Matthews swallowed her cough drop and almost choked on it.

-Yes. Gordon did change his name. If I'd known the serious nature-

-To what?

-Thomas Cooper.

Edward's eyes widened.

-What are you telling me? That he took on the same name as his foster parents' son?

-Yes.

-And, didn't you think that was kind of strange, just maybe?

-I advised against it. But, he was of age. I couldn't very well stop him. I always liked him...so soft spoken and well mannered...not like most of the other boys.

-And,?

-And, nothing.

-And, there was something you couldn't put your finger on, wasn't there? Something that you didn't like thinking about, isn't that right, Miss Matthews? Am I getting close?

Miss Matthews took a handkerchief from her purse.

-Yes. Please, Mr. Mendez, I will not theorize about that young man. It wouldn't be fair.

-What's Prentiss' background like?

-His family was killed in a car crash: mother, father and two younger sisters.

-He wasn't in the car at the time?

-He was, but somehow he got out. I believe he was thrown clear. The car collided head on into a propane tank.

-Pretty horrible way to die.

-Ghastly.

Miss Matthews shook her head and once again dipped into her pocketbook; this time, she took out a cigarette and lit up.

-Where is the new Mr. Tom Cooper today?

-I don't know. Mr. Mendez, I see we smoke the same brand. I do know that he was boarding in a rooming house somewhere in Brooklyn. I believe near the downtown shopping district. From what I gather, it was a rather seedy place.

-When was that?

-No more than two years ago. I haven't heard from him since.

-Here's my card, Miss Matthews. Please call me if you should hear from him.

-Is he in danger of any kind?

Edward grinned at the inanity of that question.

-No. *He* isn't.

Edward stopped at the first public phone booth he could find. He dialed Ginny Gray's number. She answered on the first ring.

-Ginny Gray.

-Ginny, it's Edward Mendez. I've got some news for you.

He told her about his meeting with Miss Mathews. Ginny was impressed.

-Eddie, baby, that's awesome and downright bizarre.

-That was my take on it. Okay, Ginny, now I know I've gotta' track this character down. There's gotta' be a record of his name change from Gordon Prentiss to Tom Cooper.

-Absolutely. Let ole' Ginny handle that. His birth certificate will still read "Gordon Prentiss." Now...he had to have chosen a different middle name. It's illegal to take someone else's full name.

-And, don't you have to post this in the papers for a couple of weeks?

-Thirty days to be exact. And, if no one objects, you're set to go. I'll get right on it.

-Thanks.

-And, Eddie, where are you headed for now?

-I was going to take another trip to the original Tom Cooper's place; see if I can shake him down.

-The original Tom Cooper.

-Maybe.

-What do you mean "maybe?"

-Was I talking to the original Tom Cooper?

-You mean Prentiss might have taken over his identity completely?

-Stranger things have happened.

-But where does that leave the real Tom Cooper? You don't think...

-That Prentiss bumped him off?

-Something like that, yeah.

-The thought has crossed my mind.

-You said you *were* on your way there.

-Got this call from Vegas this morning. Seems that April Keyes took a Steve Brody out there. Also sounds like she might be listed in the obituaries.

-Eddie, baby, we've gotta keep each other posted. I mean like every few hours.

-Agreed. Now, I've gotta' hang up and book a flight to Vegas. Wish me luck.

Edward had just enough time to pack an overnight bag and say a brief goodbye to his sisters Nella and Victoria. He stopped off at his office and told Dottie to expect a call from Ginny Gray at any time. Marlena Lake might also be calling.

-Eddie, our Dad called.

The P. I. did a double take.

-What did he want?

-He's got a house guest.

-Dare I ask who?

-Nathalie Montaigne. Miss French expatriate herself.

-What the heck is he up to now?

-Said to call him when you get a chance. Seems sort of urgent.

-It'll have to wait. Anything else?

Dottie hesitated.

-No. Not yet, anyway.

-Don't be so mysterious, sister. Give.

-It's a surprise.

-What kind of "surprise?"

Dottie changed the subject.

-How you getting out to Idlewild?

-Driving out. I'll park the car in the garage. And, I'd better hurry. And, what are you smiling about?

-Have a safe trip. And, watch out for those show-girls. I hear they're faster than race cars.

Edward boarded the propeller plane for Las Vegas. It would make a stopover in Chicago for refueling and then head directly to the desert city. He'd arrive there at just about sunset. He remembered the last time he had seen the sunset in the desert...the place had been Egypt and he was suffering from amnesia.

The P. I. made himself comfortable in his window seat. Passengers were still boarding. As he glanced out the window, a young woman sat down next to him.

-Do you mind very much if I sit here?

Edward didn't have to turn around to see who it was, but he did turn around anyway.

-Yolanda.

THIRTEEN

MARLENA LAKE insisted on seeing Lt. William Donovan. She wouldn't leave the Precinct House otherwise. She was sitting in the "official" coffee room Alex Raymond was with her and each woman had a cup of coffee.

-Lt. Donovan is here, Miss Lake, but he's very busy.

-So am I. Perhaps, you can help me, Miss Raymond. We are not unknown to each other, quite the contrary.

-How can I help?

-If the Lieutenant won't see me-

-I did not say that, Miss Lake.

-Then, deliver this message, if you would. The Sumerian urn is mine. I must have it back. In the wrong hands...well, it is quite a dangerous object...fatal, in fact. Look what it did to Werner Hoffman. By the way, has he been found?

-No. Not yet.

-I may be of help in locating him.

-How is that, Miss Lake?

Marlena put down her coffee cup and leaned forward in her chair.

-Werner Hoffman died. He, then, rose from the dead.

-You can't be serious.

-I am quite serious. You might find him concealed in a graveyard.

-Why in the world would he go to a graveyard? He has no mind left.

-Doesn't he, Miss Raymond? He's killed and eluded the police so far. His mind has been altered. He is what you might call the undead.

Lt. Donovan walked in.

-Miss Lake? Why don't you come into my office? I've been expecting you.

-Excellent idea. And, Miss Raymond, act quickly upon my advice while it is still daylight.

-Miss Lake?

Lt. Donovan led the way into his small but neat office.

-Please, Miss Lake have a seat. Now, let me guess why you're here: the Sumerian urn.

-Bulls eye, Lieutenant. I want it back. I *must* have it back.

-Just as soon as it's been thoroughly tested and-

-But, that must not happen; that is why I am here.

-Why not?

-You don't know what you're dealing with.

-So, what are we dealing with?

-A weapon, Lt. Donovan: a cataclysmic weapon that is capable of shattering entire cities...perhaps, even the very core of this planet.

-It didn't do any of that the other night at the museum.

-Because Werner Hoffman was incompetent. And, thank God for that small blessing. Edward Mendez stopped the urn's rotation; that is what prevented further damage.

Lt. Donovan put both hands on his desk.

-How do you know all this, Miss Lake.

-It is part of my life's work. I have always had a passion for sacred objects and things of the unknown.

-Sacred objects? And, this urn is a "sacred" object?

-Of course. It was given to us by the Anunanki; the gods who descended from heaven. It was they who gave us the keys to civilization.

-And, they left this run – this weapon – in our hands.

-Yes. It was very foolish of them.

Lt. Donovan smiled.

-I'll say!

-May I have my property back now?

-I'll see what I can do. But, Miss Lake, what are you planning to do with it, if you don't mind my asking.

-I will carefully experiment with it and treat it with the respect that it deserves. And, if that proves too dangerous, I will have it buried in the remotest of places under tons of rock and asphalt or thrown into the nearest furnace.

The Lieutenant had a thought.

-Could this thing be used as a homing device to contact this race of gods?

Marlena was impressed with this query.

-How very perceptive of you, Lieutenant. What you suggest could be dangerous to our own race. We may even contact *another* alien race...a very dangerous one...one much more highly developed than our own.

Henriette finished washing the breakfast dishes. She almost dropped a coffee cup. Last night's escape was still very much on her mind. The image of that man's face was something that she was not likely to forget. Still, she had to get to work and the morning sunlight helped to steel her nerves.

She put on her coat and hat, gathered up her handbag and made to leave for work. But, at the last minute, she had a thought: to see Edward Mendez. It would have to be a short visit to the P. I.'s office and there wasn't that much to tell him, anyway. But, she felt that it was important to tell Edward what had happened last night. And, if he wasn't in his office, she would leave a message for him.

-Oh, he is not in?

-Gone to Vegas, hon'. But, maybe, I can help you.

-Yes. I must tell someone about it.

-Dottie's the name. Sit down right here and spill your guts.

-Of course.

Henriette told Dottie her incredible story without embellishment or drama. Edward's sister listened and took notes in shorthand.

-In a word, "wow!" And, the last you saw of him was where?

-He was heading into the park. I believe his destination was the cemetery, but I can't be certain of that. It is only a guess.

Dottie looked over her notes.

-Hmm. From your description, this man resembles in more ways than one...Mr. Werner Hoffman, himself.

-The man who was injured at the museum? Edward told me about that.

-The very one.

-But, I thought he was in hospital under restraint.

-He escaped, but you and I are not supposed to know that.

-I don't understand.

-No one does, so join the club.

Dottie heaved a big sigh.

-I'll tell you, Henriette, I think you ought to go to the police with this story.

-Could you do that for me? I'll soon be up for citizenship and I don't want to jeopardize that.

-It won't jeopardize anything – if anything, just the opposite. If you like, I'll go with you.

-Yes! That would be so good of you, Miss Mendez. Would it be the 86th Precinct?

-It's Lt. Donovan's case. Weren't you and he...an item? If you don't mind my asking, that is.

-Not really. But, it could be awkward.

-Dottie will be with you. Let's go and see the good Lieutenant. I'll run interference.

-May I use your phone to tell my supervisor that I will be late?

-Sure. Help yourself.

Edward Mendez glanced at Yolanda Estravades and then turned his attention to the aerial view to his right. He took a deep breath and let it out...slowly. He turned to face his former girlfriend. My God! He couldn't think of a damned thing to say. She saved him the trouble.

-Edward? I've missed you these past few months very much. I hope you believe that, my darling.

-Give me a chance to catch my breath. Are we allowed to smoke just yet?

-I think so.

-I've been trying to cut back, you know.

-Did you miss me? Did you think about me at all?

-I'd be lying if I said I hadn't.

Edward lit up and took a deep drag on his Lucky Strike.

-So, Yolanda, baby, what are you doing here?

-I've come back to stay. Edward, I didn't love that man, not really. Do I need to say anymore?

The P. I.'s voice turned hard when he answered.

-Plenty. Aren't you afraid of the world that I live in?

-Yes. But, I want to be with you. I'll share the danger. I've shared it many times before, haven't I?

-Did my sister, Dottie, know about this little rendezvous of yours?

-She did, but don't be angry with her, It was my idea.

-I thought something was up.

-You're angry with me. I can understand that.

-I don't like being dumped, baby. I'll need time to simmer down.

-Edward? Is there someone else?

The P. I. lied.

-No. Not really.

-Please explain that...if you want to.

The P. I. evaded the question.

-I'm on a case right now and it could be dangerous. It involves a murdered woman by the name of Lorraine Keyes.

-All your cases are dangerous. Tell me about it. That's why you're going to Las Vegas, isn't it?

-Yes.

Edward related the case to Yolanda in detail. It helped to steady his nerves.

-It's interesting; the part about Gordon Prentiss changing his name to Tom Cooper. What's he up to?

-Up to no good, baby. But, if April is still alive, which I doubt, she could expose Mr. Tom Cooper for who he really is.

-What about that Miss Matthews at the foundling home. She could do that just as easily, no?

Edward smiled and put out his cigarette.

-You know, it's kind of nice to have my Girl Friday back.

-And, Edward, the part about Werner Hoffman, that's the frightening part. Do you believe the dead can be risen from their graves? I do. It's mentioned in the Bible. It was Lazarus who was raised from the dead.

-Just maybe I do, too. But, Marlena thinks that urn of hers is some sort of ancient weapon.

-Do you think Lt. Donovan will hand it over to her? He might not.

-It is her property.

-But, if it's a public danger-

-He'll probably have the science boys look it over.

-I hope he's careful with it.

-I'm thinking that the military might step in.

Yolanda smiled.

-I don't think Marlena would like that. Too bad for her.

The small propeller plane landed and the passengers disembarked. Edward and Yolanda took a cab to the hotel. Ada Lamont was waiting for them in the lobby.

-Mr. Mendez? I'm Ada Lamont. I'm the one who left that message for you about April.

-Miss Lamont? Yolanda Estravades, my Girl Friday.

-Pleased to meet you, Yolanda.

The two women exchanged brief pleasantries.

-Miss Lamont-

-Call me Ada.

-Ada, can you take us to where you left April Keyes?

-I've got my car right in the parking lot. I'm sure I can find the spot.

The three people were on the road that led to that part of town which would soon be a thriving suburb of Las Vegas. The houses had been built, but that was it: there were no lawns or fences or mail boxes...not yet.

Ada pulled up in front of one of those houses.

-This is it. I'm sure. Are we going in, Edward?

-That's why we're here, Ada.

They got out of the car and walked up to the front door. It wasn't locked.

Edward took out his revolver.

-Stand back.

He kicked in the door. There was no one inside. The house was dim in spite of the light filtering in through the windows. The sun was about to set. The P. I. signaled to the two girls to com on in.

Yolanda spoke first.

-Empty. There's no furniture, not even a light fixture.

Ada ran her finger along the window sill.

-No dust. Not a speck of it. What about the bedroom, Edward? That's where they took her, Tony and Mr. Gruesome.

Edward kicked that door in. Empty.

Ada peeked in.

-And, the bed's gone, too. They really cleaned house.

Edward had to agree with the showgirl.

-The damn place even smells clean, like it's been disinfected. It doesn't look too good for April.

Yolanda opened the bathroom door and walked in. Edward called out to her.

-Careful, baby. I haven't checked in there.

-It's okay. There's nothing in here with- Oh!

Edward and Ada rushed over.

-What is it?

-It's nothing, really. Just some bottles of alcohol in the medicine chest.

Edward maneuvered past her.

-Let's have a look. There's a half a dozen bottles of the stuff.

-What is it, hon'? Something left over from the cleaning lady?

That was Ada asking that.

-This same set up was in Lorraine Keyes' medicine chest...and Marco told me that one of Roger Lee's boys had nothing but alcohol in his bathroom.

-What did they use all that alcohol for?

-And, why so much of the stuff?

Edward popped a piece of bubble gum into his mouth.

-What does one use alcohol for...to disinfect?

Yolanda spoke.

-Were these people exposed to some kind of disease?

-That just might be it, baby, or something even worse.

Ada broke the silence.

-Now what?

-We report a missing person to the police.

-Edward, please... I'm walking a pretty thin line with the cops as it is. What with Tony's death and all... Well, you get my drift.

Yolanda addressed Edward.

-Edward, what would be the point? We couldn't tell them anything, not really.

The P. I. playfully squeezed Yolanda's arm.

-If it ended here, fine, but it doesn't. Lt. Donovan's involved in this and I've gotta' give him and the detective in charge of the case a complete update. We'd all be considered accessories if I don't.

Ada wasn't convinced, but she understood where Edward stood.

-Okay. Then, let's head back to the hotel, kids. I don't feel safe here.

Back in Ada's car, Edward tried reassuring the two girls.

-It won't take long. We don't have all that much to tell them. Why don't we head straight to the Precinct House. Ada?

-I'll drop you two off. My shift at the casino starts soon and I've missed too much time as it is. If you need me, you can find me at the roulette table or ask for my manager, Rex.

Yolanda and Edward checked in for the night. Ada had not been at the roulette table. She had not reported for work that evening. Her manager was upset and angry. He'd called her place, but got no answer. He tried several times to reach her and gotten nowhere.

Edward wasn't surprised.

-That chick took a powder. She's running scared and I'd like to know from whom.

-I don't blame her.

-Maybe, she did the right thing for herself...maybe.

-Did you hear what the Sergeant said to us?

-I was there, baby.

-He wants to call in the F.B.I.

-April crossed state lines along with her killer probably.

-What about her abductors, Edward?

-That's the sticky part. Are they based in Vegas? No one knows. Tony Montana might have filled us in on that. Was April taken out of the state? Again, no one knows. If the good Sergeant gets in touch with the F.B.I., he might just hit a brick wall. Hey, baby, why don't you order us some drinks from room service?

-Scotch and soda. You see, I remember.

Room service brought up the drinks in record time.

-We'll check out in the morning. The Sergeant knows where to contact me. But, so far, it's barely a missing persons case.

-That's a bit of luck for us.

-You said it, Yoli. Yep. I think I'm gonna call you that from now on.

-I like it.

-Good. We need to get back to New York. I want an update on that Sumerian urn and Werner Hoffman.

-What about Lorraine Keyes?

-She's mixed up in this. And, I still want to get a hold of Miss Matthews. She can help clear up one mystery.

FOURTEEN

EDWARD WAS wrong. Miss Matthews didn't show up for work the next day. It was the first time in twenty-seven years that she had missed a day of work: never late and never ill. They tried reaching her at her apartment, but no one picked up the phone. The police were notified. They arrived at her apartment house and spoke to the landlady: a middle-aged woman just under five feet tall and weighing close to 175 pounds. She led the two police officers up to Miss Matthews' apartment on the second floor.

-Not like Miss Matthews to sleep in or miss work. Always up at the crack of dawn. She's a real good tenant, mind you. Keeps to herself and always has her nose in a book.

She fitted the master key in the lock and it clicked open.

-There! That does it.

Mrs. Testa led the way into the apartment. She flicked on the light switch and screamed. The two police officers took a step back and stared at the lifeless figure of Miss Matthews hanging from a rope. The corpse stared blindly at the three figures in the room.

On the plane back to New York, Edward and Yolanda had a long talk.

-So, Yoli-

-Only you may call me that.

-That suits me just fine.

-Do they serve drinks on board?

-Sure.

Edward signaled to the stewardess.

-A whiskey and soda for me and a gin and tonic for the lady.

The P. I. turned back to his girlfriend.

-I've got a couple of theories buzzing in my head. This Lorraine Keyes investigation smacks of a diversion tactic – set up by my own father.

-Why would he do that, Edward? He gave you a retainer fee of $10,000. He must have a pretty good reason for doing that.

-To keep me busy. And, how did you know that?

-You must have told me...or maybe Dottie mentioned it. We talked about a lot of things.

Edward looked at his girlfriend and wasn't so sure that he believed her. He didn't let on or press her for a better answer.

-What was Lorraine Keyes to him? I doubt that he ever met her.

The P. I. rubbed his chin. The stewardess returned with their drinks.

-Thank you.

He took a long sip of his drink.

-So, Edward, what does he want you not to know about?

Edward grinned.

-Only one thing comes to this shamus' mind.

-What?

-That damned Sumerian urn. Now *that's* something he'd be interested in.

Yolanda had to agree with that.

-That makes sense. My God, Edward...your father and Marlena Lake in cahoots with each other. It doesn't bear thinking about.

Edward had to laugh.

-I can handle Marlena, I think. My father's a different story. I really don't know him and his code of ethics, if he even has any.

-So, who killed Miss Keyes?

-Lorraine Keyes? My P. I. gut instinct says a boyfriend...a boyfriend who works for Romo-Ark. The same man who lured her sister, April, out to Las Vegas. What a god forsaken city that is.

-I didn't much care for it either. But, Edward, Romo-Ark has a lot of employees.

-And, hitmen.

-Don't you need a name to put to the killer?

-How does Tom Cooper alias Gordon Prentiss strike you?

-It looks like a bulls eye to me. But, tell me something: where is the original Tom Cooper?

-Either in Jersey or dead with Gordon Prentiss doing an imitation of a now dead man.

But, I'm not so sure about that. Wish I had a photo of both men – now, that would help!

The plane landed at Idlewild Airport on schedule. Edward and Yolanda got in Edward's DeSoto and drove directly to his downtown office where Dottie was waiting for them. Dottie had news for the P. I. and it wasn't good.

-Miss Matthews hung herself.

-I'll bet!

-We think alike, brother mine.

-She was murdered like Lorraine and April. Too bad.

-April is dead then?

-I'd make bet on it. But, the Vegas police are investigating it.

The three people were in Edward's office.

-All three victims are from Gordon Prentiss' past: people who can identify him with certainty...people who were still alive. All three females who would know Prentiss by sheer instinct...his habits...his mannerisms.

He's eliminating them one by one. As we're getting closer to him, he's killing them off.

-But, Edward, what's his motive?

-To take over the real Tom Cooper's identity.

-But, why

The P. I. shook his head.

-Money? That's always a motive...the motive.

-That one's got my vote every time. Money!

-Mine, too, Dottie. It's almost too obvious. Edward, you don't look convinced.

-You two ladies are probably right, but how much money are we talking about? Just how much were the Cooper's worth?

Dottie answered that one.

-Well, we'll just have to do a little digging, won't we?.

-And, I'll be paying a visit to the man who said he was Tom Cooper.

The P. I. headed for New Jersey and Mr. Tom Cooper's house. He parked in the same spot, locked up and took out a cigarette.

-He's home. That boy doesn't go out much.

Edward knocked hard on the front door and waited. He knocked, again, harder, and waited. A voice answered from inside.

-Want do you want, Mr. Mendez?

-Open up, Tommy, and I'll tell you.

-I'm not feeling well. Please, leave. I can't help you.

-Open up! Damn it!

-I can't.

-Do it.

There was fear in Tom Cooper's voice. Edward knew this and changed his approach.

-Tommy? I can help. Trust me. You *are* Tom Cooper.

It was a statement and a chance to make a verification for what it was worth.

-Yes. I am.

Now, there was gratitude in Tom Cooper's voice. Edward noted this.

-Tommy, let me in, pal.

Tom released the safety chain and opened the door to the P. I.

-Good. Now, let's go in to the living room and sit down.

Edward led the way.

-Mind if I smoke?

-No. I don't care.

-Good.

Edward lit up. He looked around the living room. Neat as a pin, but not a single photograph on display.

-Tom, can I see your high school yearbook?

-Didn't graduate.

-What about grade school?

-Sure. You just wanna' make sure I am who I say I am, don't you?

-You're one step ahead of me, pal.

Tom got up, ran upstairs and brought back his grade school yearbook. He handed it to Edward. It was opened at his class photo.

-That's me in the first row.

The P. I. took a careful look at the photo and, then, at Tom. He handed Tom back his yearbook.

-That's you, all right.

-Seems like a really long time ago in a different world.

-Tom, have the police made any progress in your parents' murder?

-No. I don't think so.

The P. I. noted that answer.

-When you became of age, was your inheritance cleared?

-Some of it.

-What I mean is, did you come into possession of your parents' estate?

-I wouldn't be living in their house if I hadn't.

-Was their estate substantial?

-It was enough.

Edward put out his cigarette.

-I think I asked you this last time...

-About Gordon?

-Where is he?

-You're the private dick, you tell me.

-You're afraid of Gordon Prentiss. Why?

No response.

-He's threatened you.

Edward could see that the young man sitting across from him wanted to answer.

-Please, Mr. Mendez. He's not here...but he is here. I can't tell you anymore than that.

-You can. And, for your sake, you'd better.

-He just isn't here.

-He's threatened you. He's taken your name, Tommy.

-And, I hate the bastard for that. I'm Tom Cooper. He isn't. My parents weren't going to adopt him and he knew that. He knew it because he forced it out of me.

-Why had your parents changed their minds? April Keyes thought they were going to adopt Gordon.

-April was just a kid. Her and Lorraine were good kids. Lorraine liked Gordon. April liked me.

-So, Tom, where the hell is Gordon Prentiss?

-He gets around, but always comes back. Always.

-Why does he come back?

-Because he's now Tom Cooper.

-But, *you're* Tom Cooper.

-I can't explain his motives. He's dangerous, Mr. Mendez. He knows things. He's cunning...always was cunning.

-Why do you stay here, Tommy?

-He'd find me no matter where I went. And, I can't go to the police. I can't. And, people know me around here. They know that I'm the real Tom Cooper and not that-

-That "what," Tommy?

-Impostor.

Edward shook his head and put out his cigarette.

-Now, you're lying to me. You were going to say "murderer," weren't you? Weren't you?

Tom Cooper whispered his reply.

-Maybe.

FIFTEEN

EDWARD DROVE back to Manhattan. What was Tom Cooper hiding? Had to be something big. But, he was alive and Lorraine and April Keys weren't and neither was Miss Matthews. Was Gordon Prentiss the murderer and if so why keep Tom Cooper alive? He needed him, but for what.

The P. I. parked his car and went directly up to his office. Dottie was waiting for him.

-Bingo!

-I'm listening.

-Tom Cooper will inherit – now get this – a cool one million dollars when he comes of age...that is, when he turns thirty.

Edward slammed his sister's desk with the palm of his right hand.

-Like you just said, Dottie: "bingo!" That's why Tommy Cooper, the original, is still breathing. Gordon

Prentiss needs him to collect that million. He doesn't dare pass himself off as the original. But, Tommy Cooper's living with the Sword of Damocles hovering over his head.

Edward lit a cigarette.

-But, where did the Coopers get a hold of a cool million? Or how could they afford that kind of insurance? It ain't cheap.

Dottie sat back.

-Eddie, can I bum a cigarette off of you?

-Here you go.

He extended the pack of cigarettes to her.

-So, Eddie, where is Gordon Prentiss? And, why hasn't Tom Cooper gone to the police?

-Too scared. And, he's hiding something...something big.

-Like what? I'll listen to a wild guess.

-His parents, Dottie. Somehow, this is all tied in with Mr. and Mrs. Cooper. And, I suspect with the late Mr. and Mrs. Keyes...maybe to a lesser extent. The Keyes were ordered out of their house fifteen years ago. Why? And, who did the ordering? The Coopers had a million bucks in insurance or capital. Where did they get their hands on that kind of money?

Dottie took a drag on her cigarette.

-More background work? I'm all set to go.

-Good. You check out the Coopers. There's a lot of media coverage on that. I was a teenager and I remember it.

-You're gonna' take the Keyes so-called car accident?

-You bet. Who were they? What's their story?

-Oh, by the way, Susan Broder called. She said it was about that Sumerian urn. And...now don't yell at me. Promise?

-No.

-In all this hubbub, it slipped my mind: Henriette Miller came here yesterday and...

Dottie related all the events to her brother.

-Man! I'll tell you what; I'm gonna' head on over to Henriette's library. And, I might just be walking home with her tonight.

-What about the Keyes sisters?

-That's still on. I'll be back.

-Eddie, why not call Lt. Donovan. He can tell you what Henriette and I can't – like whether or not they found Werner Hoffman.

Edward thought about if for a half second.

-You're right. And, again, I was almost sidetracked.

-Again?

-Yes. This whole Lorraine Keyes case is legit, but a diversion.

-From what?

-From that damned Sumerian urn. I'm gonna' call Donovan.

-Good afternoon, Lt. William Donovan. Edward Mendez, here.

-Hello, Edward Mendez. What's up?

-That was my question for you. In a word: Hoffman.

Lt. Donovan was torn between laughing and letting our a huge and exasperated sigh.

-He's dead, again.

Edward did laugh.

-That's what we thought the first time around.

-Well, what my men found was a rotting and stinking corpse near your family mausoleum.

-My family mausoleum?

-Right on the very steps.

-And, this time he is dead, for sure?

-Unless he can pull himself together.

-You mean he's undergone an autopsy?

-He has by Dr. Claire Ingram herself. She manages to get a hold of these cases. Must be a hobby of hers.

-She's good at her job.

-I know she is and so does she. I'm not arguing with you, Mendez.

-Do you have the results?

-Some. She's not through with the cadaver just yet.

-And?

-He's been dead at least seventy-two hours.

-But, Henriette Miller saw him less than twenty-four hours ago. He was walking and with a destination in mind – that is, if he *had* a mind.

-We've got Miss Miller's statement. She's a credible witness. So, Mendez, what happened out in Vegas? Find April Keyes?

-No. Not a trace of her. The Vegas police are on it.

Edward told the Lieutenant the entire story.

-So, Mendez, where do you go from here? You think Tom Cooper and Gordon Prentiss are involved in this?

-More Gordon Prentiss. You know I can't find a single snapshot of the character; not at the Cooper place and not at that foundling home. I'm thinking of escorting Tom Cooper to your Precinct. Maybe, you can get a composite drawing of Prentiss out of him.

-It's an idea. But, there's no one around to identify him?

-No one who I know is alive.

-I know that Matthews dame is dead, but there's gotta' be someone there or who *was* there who remembers Prentiss.

-I'll keep looking into that end of it. You're right, though; somebody's gotta' be left alive who remembers what the bastard looks like.

-But, Mendez, he was involved in that double murder in Jersey. His photo should have made it into the papers.

-Maybe not. He and Cooper were minors at the time.

-But, someone at the police station there or someone in the court house would remember him.

-I'll put Dottie on to it, but don't get your hopes up. This boy knows how to hide himself. But first, I want to talk to Miss Henriette Miller.

-Good luck. And, keep me posted.

-Just a second.

-What is it?

-Maybe, I'll have a word with Dr. Claire Ingram. Whatever she's found out, you can bet your life it'll be definite and made of Roman concrete.

-So, Dr. Ingram, how does a dead man walk?

-He doesn't, Mendez. We all know that. Medically speaking, Mr. Hoffman...

-Yes?

-Yes. He was the walking dead: a sort of zombie, if you would.

Edward smiled and popped a piece of bubble gum into his mouth.

-A zombie?

-You didn't hear me say that.

-Why was he found at my family's mausoleum?

-That's more your line of investigation than mine.

-Touche. Anyway, he couldn't have been dead.

-I'm theorizing now; but a part of the brain must have still been intact. It propelled him forward toward a rather fitting destination. I honestly can't explain it. It was as if he were being summoned to his destination.

-Summoned by whom?

-Again, Mendez, that falls into your line of work. I can tell you this: he wouldn't have been going anywhere much longer.

-How do you mean?

-The bones and muscles were in a state of advanced atrophy; rigor mortis is the colloquial term. The internal organs were in a state of decay and that includes the heart and lungs. Werner Hoffman was a walking cadaver kept in motion by some type of brain stimulation. Something within the brain cortex was still functioning...exerting pressure and causing some kind of momentum.

-Pressure, Dr. Ingram, like in vibration?

-Yes. Why do you say that, Mendez? I know about the Sumerian urn business, by the way.

-Bulls eye Doctor. And, this P. I. is just starting to connect the dots. I'll be back for your full report. And, thanks.

Henriette Miller was placing one final book from the cart into its proper place on to the bookshelf.

-Finished for the day, Henriette?

-Oh, Mr. Mendez. Hello.

-It's Edward.

-Yes. I just have to check out. I won't be a minute.

Out on the sidewalk, Edward and Henriette stopped to talk. It was just about dusk and the weather was cold but dry and crisp with no wind.

-Lt. Donovan told me about your experience last night.

-I've never been so afraid in my life. Edward, I could almost smell the decay coming from Mr. Hoffman.

-Did he say anything or make any kind of sound?

-No. I can't say that he did, but he seemed to be in pain and struggling to get somewhere. I had to run to get out of his way.

-Did you see his face?

-Only from my kitchen window. Terrible. Pale and almost translucent. His clothes hung on his body like loose rags.

-And, he was headed for the cemetery?

-He was headed for the park. The cemetery is right next to it.

Edward was silent.

-Edward, what is it?

-How the devil did he get from upper Manhattan and into Brooklyn without being spotted?

-Yes! I wondered about that myself. Perhaps, someone was helping him.

-Maybe. But, who?

-We may never know.

-But, Henriette, it's my job to know.

The P. I. dropped Henriette off at the elevated train stop. And, then, another name popped into his head: Nathalie Montaigne. Werner Hoffman may have gone to her for help. They'd been friends and business associates for years and both traveled in the same occult circles. She might know how to help him.

The P. I. got into his DeSoto and drove the short distance across town to their bookshop. He parked right in front of it, got out of his car and knocked on the door. No answer. He knocked, again, careful not to damage the glass panel. He tried the handle and the door opened.

Edward entered the darkened store. All the lights were switched off. He stood in the doorway.

-Anyone here? Nathalie Montaigne?

No answer.

Edward looked for a light switch. He found it and turned the overhead lights on. Once again, he called out.

-Anyone at home?

No answer.

He walked further into the bookstore taking out his gun. Not a sound to be heard, so he kept walking further toward the back where the small kitchen was located.

The P. I. switched on the light. Nothing looked out of place. He checked the refrigerator. Empty. The cupboards were empty except for some spilled salt and quite a lot of it.

Edward walked back to the front of the store, checking bookshelves for any disruptions. He found none. He checked behind the counter and took the liberty of ringing up the cash register. And, it was empty except for some loose change. He slammed it shut, closed the lights and left.

-Hoffman was here. He took money and...salt.

He was about to walk back to his car when the name "Nathalie Montaigne" caught his eye. He pressed the call buzzer not expecting to get an answer. He got no answer. He stepped back a few feet and saw that no lights were on in her apartment.

A darkened apartment with no sign of its occupant.

A bookshop left open and unattended.

They knew where Werner Hoffman was.

Where was Natalie Montaigne?

-Dearest Manuel, I do so love your place. It is quite comfortable without being ostentatious.

-Much of that is owed to its former Mistress, Miranda Drake.

-And, what has become of Miss Drake, cherie?

-She is deceased. Hers is a complex tale. A woman who ventured into dangerous knowledge...a woman who shouldn't have.

-The occult, one would assume.

-Quite.

-Yes. One must be careful, there are many traps along that dark path.

Manuel Mendez put down his coffee.

-You and Werner Hoffman are occultists.

-Yes, but we are not devoted wholeheartedly to it. There is safety in the pedestrian side of life.

-I agree that it can offer a rather safe if inconsistent haven.

Nathalie placed her coffee cup on the end table.

-Dear Manuel, why I am here?

-You come straight to the purpose.

-Is there another way?

Manuel laughed at his guest's question.

-I am forming a new coven; a circle, if you would, of occultists.

-An enclave?

-You may put it that way. Our purpose will be power and our methods will be ruthless.

-Power to what end?

-Wealth and influence.

-And the method?

-The Sumerian urn.

-Ah! Now, I understand. But, Manuel, it is so very dangerous to use. Look at what happened to Werner. Ghastly!

-Only an Anunanki or an occultist may use that instrument with any degree of safety.

-But, Werner was an occultist.

-An amateur as you yourself admitted...a bumbling amateur who overrated his abilities. I am neither an amateur nor a fool.

-And, who are these Anunanki? The term is somewhat familiar to me.

-The ancient ones who came down from the wandering planet. But, they need not concern us.

-How will we use this urn?

-In a ritual format.

-And, its energy will be directed at whom?

Manuel got up and walked over to the fireplace.

-When, did you ask?

-There will be a target, no doubt...a victim. I am not naive, cherie.

-If you were, you wouldn't be sitting here, much less taken into my confidence.

-And? You haven't answered my question.

-A target: that will be significant. What about St. Patrick's Cathedral?

-That would anger a great many people not to mention the powers that control it.

-You may be right about that. An alternate plan, then...say the Chrysler Building in midtown Manhattan? Yes. To see it shatter into dust and the beautiful art-deco roof come crashing down into the street.

Nathalie Montaigne was starting to feel uneasy. This man's plans were fantastic. And how could he hope to carry them out?

-And, how does one direct the urn's power?

-Through the mind of the triangle of manifestation.

-And, who would be this third party?

-I have several prospects in mind.

-Who are they, Manuel. You must tell me.

-My son-

-Never! Never would he consent to such a thing.

-A pity. How about Marlena Lake?

-Perhaps, But, I have my doubts about her, as well. You are toying with me. Who do you really have in mind?

-Mr. Roger Lee.

-Wasn't he involved in that kidnapping incident with Susan Broder?

-He was my hired accomplice.

-So, it was you behind Susan Broder's kidnapping. How very clever. Has Mr. Lee consented?

-He will. I've merely to place a single call to Mr. Lee. And, there is another-

The doorbell rang. Manuel's manservant went to answer it. He came back into the Drawing Room.

-It's your son, Mr. Edward Mendez.

-See him in, please.

Manuel turned to Nathalie.

-Are you up to this?

-Of course. I like your son.

-I'm not so sure that I do.

SIXTEEN

LT. DONOVAN and Marlena Lake were sitting in the Lieutenant's office on the third floor of the 86th Precinct. Both people were regarding each other in a rather unfavorable light.

The Lieutenant thought of Miss Lake as a pompous ass, at best and at worst, as a criminal who should be placed behind bars. He knew that she was an occultist with a rather shady background. Several years ago, thefts had been reported by various churches and synagogues. Miss Lake and her now deceased son had come under suspicion, but their proof of guilt had been circumstantial. And, of course, there had been the murder of Dolores Sarney who'd been a friend of Yolanda Estravades. Miss Sarney's body had been fished out of the river: disemboweled of several internal organs. Miss Estravades and Miss Lake claimed complete ignorance of the matter. Lt. Donovan did not believer either woman.

He reached for the pack of cigarettes on his desk and lit up.

Miss Lake despised Lt. Donovan. An incompetent police officer who relied far too much on his minions and Edward Mendez. She didn't like his attitude toward her one bit. How dare he feel superior to her? Who in hell was he? But, one thing was in the Lieutenant's favor. Yes. The urn was lying on his desk in full view. All she had to do now was sign the release form to claim her property. How easy it had been to reclaim it from these fools. Their so-called technicians didn't have a clue as to how to work it. Their conclusion regarding the urn: it was an antique!

Marlena could barely hide her incredulity at such a conclusion. And, what of Werner Hoffman? The urn and his "attack" were unrelated.

-Miss Lake?

-Oh, pardon me, Lieutenant. I was lost in my own musings. Where do I sign?

-On the dotted line.

-She signed the release form and placed the urn, carefully, in her over-sized pocketbook.

-Would you like an escort home, Miss Lake?

-How very chivalrous of you, Lt. Donovan, to offer.

-Your carrying a priceless antique on your person.

-I am, aren't I?

-Miss Lake, what will you do with it now?

-Admire it. Research its history.

-Anything else?

-What are you getting at, Lieutenant.

As if she didn't know.

-Remember, Miss Lake, I was at the museum and saw first hand what it did to poor Werner Hoffman.

-There may have been more to that incident than met the eye. I'm still puzzled at how an experienced occultist such as Mr. Hoffman could have been so careless if not downright stupid. I would have given the man more credit than that.

-He could have been nervous about handling it.

-But, he was prepared. He must have laid careful plans in advance. I must speak to his woman friend, Nathalie Montaigne.

-Miss Montaigne. Just the person I was looking for. Thanks for saving me the trouble.

-How very flattering, cherie.

-Your bookshop was open. I had a look around.

Nathalie sat upright in her chair at this news.

-Open, you say? But, I remember locking up.

-Nothing seemed to be amiss; but the cash register had been emptied.

Nathalie, once again, sat back in her chair.

-I did that. I needed the ready cash. But, the door should have been locked. I must go there tomorrow morning and see things for myself.

Edward turned to his father.

-I didn't know that you two knew each other?

-The occult circles overlap, Edward. What brings you here?

-Mr. Werner Hoffman is dead. He was spotted headed for the cemetery at Highland Park. He was found lying prone on the steps of the Mendez mausoleum.

Manuel Mendez raised an eyebrow.

-Curious. I can't imagine why he'd go there of all places.

-I think you do know why, father.

-I don't. But to stay within the same framework, where is the urn? Do the police still have it?

-Not if Marlena Lake has anything to say about it.

Nathalie laughed.

-That one will get it back one way or another. She has quite the reputation.

Manuel Mendez also laughed.

-Yes. I'll be rooting for her.

He stopped laughing.

-By the way, Edward, how is the Lorraine Keyes investigation coming along? Any progress to report?

-Yes. But, I'm not at liberty to say.

-Not even to me? I'm the one financing your investigation, young man.

-Yes, father, I know. And, I'm still wondering why.

-Have you made any substantial progress in the case?

-Yes. I've made progress.

-Suspects?

-One in particular.

-I won't press you for details.

-Father? Can you tell me anything about that Sumerian urn?

-I would like to possess it.

-Fat chance. Marlena's not going to give it up.

-She needn't "give it up."

-What do you know about it?

-I know its history, young man.

-And?

-And, I know how to use it. You see, Edward? I can be as enigmatic as you.

-When do you plan on using it?

-Did I mention anything about plans? To answer my own question, I did not. Don't be so presumptuous. And, now if you will excuse Nathalie and myself? We've things to discuss.

Edward grinned and made to leave.

-And, plans to make? Goodbye, father. Miss Montaigne?

SEVENTEEN

IT WAS a Friday morning and cold outside. Edward sat at his desk with two distinct thoughts running through his detective's brain.

The first thought was of Lorraine Keyes. He had a suspect and a motive for her murder. The suspect was Gordon Prentiss. The motive was the identifying of Gordon Prentiss. Lorraine and April Keyes, who was presumed dead, could identify Gordon Prentiss...and so could Miss Matthews. They had to be eliminated. But, Tom Cooper had to stay alive to collect his inheritance; an inheritance that Gordon Prentiss intended to collect probably through blackmail or eventual murder. Tom Cooper could help Edward's investigation, but would not out of fear...or was there another reason? But, putting all that aside, where was Gordon Prentiss? Was he working for Romo-Ark? Edward couldn't shake that suspicion out of his head. But...Gordon Prentiss would have to stay close to Tom Cooper...watch him...check up on him...to make certain that his gravy train didn't skip town.

The second thought was about the Sumerian urn and what his father was up to. Edward didn't care for his new friend, Nathalie Montaigne: a disreputable person if ever there was on.

And, then, it hit the P. I. He reached for the phone and dialed the 86th Precinct.

-Miss Alex Raymond, please.

Edward waited. In the meantime, he lit a cigarette.

-Alex Raymond, here.

-Alex? Edward Mendez. How are you?

-Not too bad. How about yourself? I hear that Yolanda's back in town.

-Man, that grapevine is faster than the damned speed of light.

-Isn't it? And, Edward, have you heard the latest?

-Fill me in.

-April Keyes was found dead in that house that you investigated. Her body was found int the basement, strangled.

-I was afraid of that. But, Alex, there was no basement in that house.

-Apparently, there was. That's where the body *was* found. She'd been strangled, Edward...and brutally beaten.

-I don't know what to say. I checked that entire place. Man! Where was this "house?"

-In one of the upcoming suburbs just a few miles from the city.

-That sounds about right. I guess I'll just have to accept it. Maybe, Ada Lamont got her houses mixed up. They all kind of looked alike. Any suspects?

-It's an ongoing investigation, but they're looking for Ruby Lamont and they'd like to hear from you, as well.

-I'll give them a call. But, Alex, I do need a favor. Did you make any contacts at Romo-Ark when you were doing undercover work there? I got a couple of leads from Ginny Gray.

-Let me think for a second. A couple of secretaries, but I'm not too sure that I'd trust them. Okay, Edward, a nice guy down in the mail room. He's all right. What do you want me to get out of him?

-A name and location: Tom Cooper formerly Gordon Prentiss and where he's calling home these days.

-I'll get right on it. Bill filled me in on some of the details. Give me twelve hours or less.

-You've got it. And, thanks, Alex.

-Don't mention it. And, give my regards to Yolanda.

Edward smiled at that little joke.

-Yolanda Estravades is back in town?

Marlena didn't wait for Susan to answer.

-It doesn't really matter, does it? Her coffee planter boyfriend probably dumped her.

-Or vice versa.

-I don't care about the circumstances. The fact is: she's back. And, probably has her claws into Edward.

-Now, mother, you don't know that.

-Don't I? Is she still skating?

-I've no idea. Does it matter?

-She might fall through the ice and drown.

Marlena smiled at that last thought.

-Mother, don't you have more important things to worry about?

Marlena ignored her daughter's question.

-What about his new girlfriend, a Miss Jamie Farley? What of her?

-What about her? And, I don't think Edward was seeing much of her.

-I rather liked the girl. She had a sense of style about her.

-Really, mother... You did not like her in the least.

-I disliked her less than that ice skater.

-Well, that wouldn't be too difficult. You despise Yolanda.

-Anyway...as you just pointed out, dear, I have far more important things on my mind.

-Like your Sumerian urn, mother?

-Quite.

Marlena sat down in one of the armchairs.

-Susan, how long has it been since we've held a proper ritual?

-A couple of years, at least. Not since that ghastly episode in Egypt.

-It's been far too long. We'll have to correct that.

-And, who will be the participants?

-Oh, myself, of course. You...

-And, Edward Mendez?

-Possibly or even Manuel Mendez.

-And, the purpose of this ritual? Or should I say toward what end?

-Well put, dear. Frankly, I'm not certain. Perhaps, as an experiment of sorts.

-I don't believe you, mother.

Marlena smiled at her daughter.

-You know me all too well, Susan. I leave nothing to chance.

Roger Lee was having his breakfast at a diner that he owned in Chinatown. He'd had it refurbished and modernized to suit the clientele that he hoped to attract. He was still "underground," although some of the "heat" was off because of his cooperation with Edward Mendez and Lt. Donovan. In Chinatown, he moved about freely and conducted his business as usual without fear of police interference. He was a man who was feared and respected. His nightclubs were his main source of legitimate income and helped to launder his drug money. Opium was precious: "powdered gold," he liked to call it. A narcotic that never went out of style.

He finished his second cup of coffee, a beverage that he was gradually acquiring a taste for. It would never replace tea, but it was a decent enough substitute.

A man walked into the diner and sat at Roger Lee's table. Mr. Lee was annoyed. He valued his privacy.

-You want something, pal?

And, then, it struck him that he knew this man. He was Manuel Mendez's manservant.

-My master has sent me looking for you.

-How the hell did you find me? How did you know where to look.

-I didn't. It's been several days that I have been tracking you down, so to speak. My knowledge of Chinatown has increased ten-fold.

-Good for you. What does your Master want?

-You come straight to the heart of the matter. He would like to meet with you. You've not been answering your phone, Mr. Lee.

-Maybe, I don't want to meet with him.

-My master understands your caution. He will arrange for transport.

-What's this meeting about?

-He will tell you that.

Roger Lee grinned.

-Always "cloak and dagger" with your so called Master. There had better be a payoff.

-The "payoff," as you so quaintly put it will be $100,000.

Roger Lee was impressed in spite of himself. But, what was the risk? Had to be pretty high to earn that kind of money. But, why not? He was a gambler with plenty of nerve.

-Okay. Tell your "Master" that I'm in. Here's where you can reach me.

He handed the manservant a business card.

-And, there better not be a double-cross. I know that Manuel Mendez is dangerous, but so am I.

-Hello, Edward? Alex Raymond calling back.

Edward smiled into the receiver.

-That was fast.

-I'm very efficient. Yes. Tom Cooper does work for Romo-Ark. Has been for the past two years.

-As what, Alex? A hitman?

-That would be my guess. He works for Security, so he has a license to carry a gun.

-Lorraine's throat was slit. April was beaten and strangled.

-A much quieter way to kill someone.

-You're right about that. And, I'm sure Romo-Ark has been training him in the art of the kill.

-It's one of their specialties.

-And, he's still with them?

-As far as my source can find out.

-Hmm.

-What is it, Eddie?

-The Lorraine Keyes murder smells more like a personal vendetta...something not sanctioned by Romo-Ark. He may be on the outs with his employer. Any clue, Alex, as to where he lives or calls home?

-No. Security personnel has no home address or phone number. They're an entity on to themselves.

Edward thought about this for a second.

-Then, it's back to the original Tom Cooper's home.

-Looks like it. Eddie, let me know how you make out. Maybe, I can help.

-You bet. And, thanks, Alex.

The P. I. went to talk with Dottie. He filled her in on the latest. She was just getting off the phone and putting a newspaper clipping into a folder.

-Well, brother, did you know that Tom Cooper and Gordon Prentiss were – and still are – prime suspects in the New Jersey murders of Cooper's parents?

-I thought that they were pretty much cleared. They had an alibi for each other and there was practically no circumstantial evidence on either one of them.

-They had an alibi with the help of those two murdered girls. So...where is Mr. Prentiss who now calls himself Mr. Cooper?

-Beats the hell out of me, Dottie. Could still be in Las Vegas, if he was ever there.

-You think he might have an accomplice: a fellow hitman from Romo-Ark?

-Could be. But, I doubt it. Prentiss was always a loner. Didn't make friends.

-He was friends with Tom Cooper.

-Friends, Dottie, or a convenient ally?

The P. I. didn't wait for an answer.

-I'm gonna have to pay Tom Cooper another visit. He's probably sick of the sight of me by now.

-You think he'll talk?

-He was starting to unravel. He's scared and scared men crack.

-So, when does he come of age to inherit all that money?

-Just three days from now. If it's the inheritance that Prentiss is after, then Cooper's safe for the next three days, at least. And, I'll bet my bottom buck that he knows where Prentiss is or at least can point me in the general direction.

-And, what about this Sumerian urn business?

-Marlena is up to her neck in that one.

-Which spells intrigue and trouble.

-That, you can say, again!

Yolanda Estravades sat at her kitchen table in her Manhattan apartment. Her buttered toast was still untouched and her coffee, black with no sugar, was getting cold. The day outside was sunny and brisk and just maybe she would go for a walk in Washington Square Park later on. But, right now she was waiting for Edward to call her as she knew he would. Last night was proof of that. He'd spent the night with her. It was all part of her plan to be a complete part of his life, again.

She appreciated the fact that he had maintained her apartment: paid the rent and the utilities. And, the place was spotless. But, Yolanda knew that another girl had entered his life. Her name was Jamie Farley and she was very pretty...too pretty. Her informant had told her all about this new girl and how Edward, for the moment, was keeping her at a distance. Good. Very good. Her informant had also told her of the P. I.'s time travel adventure and how he and others had succeeded in changing history. How she wished that she'd been a part of that.

-My boyfriend is very talented. And, now I am back to stay.

Yolanda's break up with her Brazilian fiance had not been an amicable one; and that was putting it on its best terms. Mr. Jores Chacon lived on the precipice of bankruptcy. A beautiful wife, a medal winning figure skater, would boost his status in the community and with his creditors. His family tolerated Yolanda, but no more than that. Their animosity was palpable. And, once again, her informant had alerted her to all of this.

Yolanda broke off the engagement. Mr. Chacon was furious. How dare she have any knowledge of his finances? He threatened to keep her there by force. Yolanda didn't give him that chance. On a shopping trip to Rio, she alluded her companions, hailed a taxi and went straight to the airport, leaving everything behind: her jewelry...her clothes...except what she carried on her person and in her handbag: $500 in Brazilian currency, her passport and a few cosmetics. When she arrived in New York, she had only $100 left. She went straight to her informant for more money. He was generous. Now she had $10,000 in her new bank account.

-It pays to have good connections.

Her phone started ringing.

EIGHTEEN

IT WAS getting closer to that inheritance day and Gordon Prentiss, who now called himself Tom Cooper, was worried. As a matter of fact, he was sweating profusely under the armpits. They must have suspected him of murdering Lorraine Keyes by now. If he were in the cops' place, he'd be their number one suspect. Prentiss remembered April and Lorraine as two cute little kids. When they were gone from his life, he missed them even though it was he who had killed them. Well...he killed Lorraine and sent Jack Dana to kill April.

Prentiss had met Jack Dana at Romo-Ark who was a loner and angry man like himself. The tow of them had a good working relationship, but carried it no further than that. Mr. Dana had merely done Mr. Prentiss a professional favor and Mr. Cooper was now in his debt.

And, now, what was his next move? He almost knew, but didn't want to admit it to himself. Should he contact Edward Mendez? And, tell the P. I. what? No. Best not to go that route. He wasn't about to commit suicide...not for anyone. Why set the P. I. on a false trail that might bring him closer to Tom Cooper? The shamus was close enough to the truth as it was.

Gordon Prentiss made an about face and headed toward the connecting New Jersey transit. Better to face adversity head on. He'd be absent from work for the first time since his employment at Romo-Ark – not exactly a nine-to-five job – which was right up his alley. A desk job for him would never do. He didn't have the temperament for it. He was not one to tolerate the petty foibles of others. He was a loner by choice and desire and always had been. The one man who had almost been his friend...who could have been his friend...was Tom Cooper. But, not anymore. He hated Tom Cooper. He had taken his very name to annoy the living hell out of him...to confuse the bastard and keep him off balance.

Gordon Prentiss checked his gun. A good hitman always checked his weapon. He was sweating less and feeling better. A destination...even a dangerous one...was part of his job; a job that he was very good at.

-It's time that I laid my plans out.

-I thought you had already done that, cherie.

-The date is set and the "example" will be executed.

-And, the ransom price?

-One hundred million and complete immunity. Think of it, Nathalie. I will be giving the United States government an offensive weapon never even dreamt of...at least not in this ear.

-You know, cherie, you could sell it to the highest bidder. Many would pay even a higher price for such an object.

-I've considered that. And, if my demand is not met, it will go to the highest badder. We think alike.

Nathalie buttered the last of her toast.

-Two questions for you, Manuel.

-What are they?

-Where will the ritual take place?

-At the Mendez mausoleum.

-How appropriate.

-And, your second question?

-The urn, how do you plan on getting it from Marlena Lake?

-By invitation.

-To the ritual.

-Yes. I know her and she will not refuse such an invitation.

-And, you plan to steal it from her.

-That wasn't a question, was it? If I must, I will have no compunction in killing her to get it.

-That will not be so easy. She is a woman of resources who can defend herself.

-Not against me.

-Don't be so over confident, Manuel. Because she is a woman, do not make the mistake in underestimating her. And, your son is a good friend of Miss Lake's.

-I know of that unholy alliance.

-Who else will be at this ritual?

-Roger Lee. He will do anything for money.

-Who else?

-Marlena. And, perhaps, her daughter, Susan. Maybe...even Edward and his girlfriend.

-Jamie Farley? She doesn't seem the type.

Manuel's smile was not so nice.

-No, Nathalie. Yolanda Estravades. And, she is the type.

-She is back in town?

-To stay.

Manuel got up and walked about the room.

-And, now, I must visit Miss Lake. And, in a few days, issue a warning to Lt. William Donovan. It will be a warning that the good Lieutenant had better take seriously. The Chrysler building in midtown Manhattan will be demolished. If my demands are met, however, no further destruction will ensue.

-And, if your demands are not met?

-The entire city will be turned to rubble and dust...after it has been evacuated, of course. I am not a mass murderer.

-Why Lt. Donovan? Why not the Mayor, himself?

-The Mayor is a fool. Lt. Donovan is all too familiar with the occult. He has first hand knowledge of it. And, he is intimately aware of the Sumerian urn. He will take the threat seriously.

-And, cherie?

-And, he knows Edward. They are not overly fond of each other, but a mutual respect does exist between the two men.

Nathalie shook her head.

-You doubt my plans? I can see that you do.

-Such grandiose plans and, yet, you do not have the urn!

-We have a few days more...more than enough time.

Edward went back into his office, sat down, took out a cigarette and lit up. Lorraine Keyes' body had been released, but no one had come forward to claim it. Her only living relative was in a Las Vegas morgue

The P. I. needed help with this case. He had to find Gordon Prentiss and he couldn't do all the legwork by himself. He picked up the phone and dialed the 86th Precinct.

-Marco Morales, please. Edward Mendez calling.

-The P. I. waited.

-Marco Morales here. Eddie?

-It's Eddie, Marco. I'll cut straight to it. I need you for surveillance work.

-Let me guess, man: Tom Cooper's place in Jersey.

-Bulls eye. That police grapevine is faster than a Fighter Jet.

-A lot faster.

-Marco, can you get out there now?

-As a matter of fact, I'm just going off duty. Give me the address, man. This is one interesting case.

-You're a gem, Marco.

Edward hung up the phone and was about to put out his cigarette when Dottie walked in.

-Eddie, you have a visitor.

-A client?

-Not too sure. Name's Miss Ashton Bennett.

-Ashton Bennett...that name rings a distant bell. Ask her to come in. I'll straighten my necktie.

Three seconds later, Miss Ashton Bennett walked into Edward's office. Edward got up to greet her.

-Miss Bennett? Please, have a seat.

-Thank you, Mr. Mendez.

Miss Ashton Bennett looked as if she had just stepped out of the cover of Vogue magazine. The up-swept platinum hair...the high sculpted cheek bones and model slim figure. And, those violet eyes were almost hypnotic. Edward recognized the perfume: Joy. Susan Broder used the same fragrance.

-Miss Bennett, what can I do for you?

-That's a difficult question to answer. I have come about the Sumerian urn.

Edward sat back and smiled.

-Everyone and their Aunt Mary wants that urn – myself included. Why do you want it, Miss Bennett?

-My father, Mr. Mendez, is an archaeologist, a very noted archaeologist.

-Yes! I knew that last name rang a bell: Professor Bernard Bennett. Wasn't he part of the Howard Carter expedition to King Tut's tomb?

-He was. And, it nearly cost him his life.

-How do you mean?

-You've not heard of King Tut's curse, Mr. Mendez?

-I have, but I don't give it any credence.

-You should.

-Miss Bennett, what happened to your father?

-He contracted malaria. It nearly killed him.

-Is that so uncommon?

-No. It isn't. However, on the heels of his recovery, he contracted still another disease.

-In your father's weakened state, that might even have been expected.

-This disease had no name. It paralyzed him for weeks...and then it disappeared as mysteriously as it had appeared. His body, Mr. Mendez, was rigid...as rigid as stone or as if rigor mortis had set in. At first, we actually thought he was dead.

-Do you mind if I smoke?

-Not at all.

-Tell me, Miss Bennett, what does this have to do with the Sumerian urn?

-It's part of antiquity

-That doesn't answer my question.

-I'm sorry. The Sumerian and Egyptian cultures are much older than standard textbooks have recorded them. That particular urn is Sumerian, but it was found near the ancient city of Memphis in Egypt. It shouldn't have been there, but it was. The Sumerian civilization was in decline. The urn must have been taken by marauders. My father unearthed that urn, Mr. Mendez. He'd completed his work with Mr. Carter and had moved on to another dig. It was in the ruins near Memphis that the urn was found and, then, stolen from him.

-Who stole it, Miss Bennett?

-I suspect an acquaintance of yours.

-"Suspect?"

-My father did not actually see it stolen, but Marlena Lake had visited the site and when she left, the urn was missing.

Edward put out his cigarette.

-When was this?

-A little over three years ago.

Edward nodded his head. The timing was just about right. And, it's something that he wouldn't put past Marlena. But, had she lost the urn or had it in turn been taken from her?

-Your story holds up, Miss Bennett.

-You must be wondering why it's taken three years for the urn to resurface.

-Frankly, yes.

-Miss Lake was more than likely unaware of its inherent dangers.

-That, Miss Bennett, is unlikely.

-Or she was forced to hand it over to an Egyptian dealer who was backed by his government. They wouldn't be above using force or at the very least threats. Miss Lake would have to hand the urn over to them or face jail.

The P. I. finished the narrative for Miss Bennett.

-And, waited for an opportunity to get it back. Oh, Miss Bennett, we've seen what that urn can do.

-You *think* you have.

Miss Bennett leaned forward in her chair.

-Mr. Mendez, that urn can shatter this very planet.

Detective Marco Morales was parked down the block from Tom Cooper's house. He'd been there for over an hour which was not very long for a stake-out. He was a patient and observant man who didn't miss very much in the way of detail. And, he was always eager to help out his friend, Edward Mendez.

The area that he was in was quiet and residential. It was just on the outskirts of Jersey City and had an almost rural quality to it. Officer Morales appreciated the quality of the area, but not its location. It was too far from the center of the city.

And, then, he saw a figure of a man walking toward Cooper's house. He was tall, just under six feet, and had a slim but athletic build. Was that Gordon Prentiss? Marco would give better than even odds that it was. The man took out a set of keys and let himself into Tom Cooper's house.

Marco got out of his car, crossed the street and walked toward Cooper's house. He walked by the house but couldn't see anyone inside. He kept walking until he reached the corner, made a sharp right and walked down that block until he reached that corner house's backyard. Marco made a b-line across that back-yard, jumped the picket fence, crossed over that house's backyard to find himself behind Tom Cooper's house.

Marco crouched down beneath a back window and heard voices coming from inside.

-The day after tomorrow and we'll have it made. Happy Birthday, Tom, you'll be thirty years old.

-We'll have money, you mean.

-Like I just said, we'll have it made.

-It's taken long enough. Too damned long.

-Not as long as it would have taken.

-Don't remind me.

-Just maybe you need reminding. I've cleared the road, pal, just remember that.

-Maybe there was a better way...a more humane way.

-Tell me about it. I want to hear.

Silence.

-Thought so. Potential witnesses that could put a hat pin in our story. Memories have a bad way of coming back to haunt you. You know I'm right.

The voices moved into another room. Marco could still hear the voices, but couldn't make out any words. He went back the way he came. He now had a pretty good idea of who had killed Lorraine and April Keyes and why: money. The detective hurried back to his car and headed for Manhattan.

-Miss Bennett, this urn...oughtn't it to be destroyed if it can do all that you're telling me?

-Yes, Mr. Mendez, but not haphazardly...certainly not with a sledge hammer.

-I wasn't thinking along those lines. Please, give me a little credit.

-Within the urn, there are components that our own science hasn't caught up with yet. It was unearthed in a city that had been built by the Sumerians. The urn was encased within a stone receptacle that was lined in gold plate. It should be returned or destroyed ...carefully.

-Well, I know where it is. Somehow, Marlena Lake has gotten it back.

-She's playing with fire, Mr. Mendez. Please, get it back from her.

-I just can't take it from her, Miss Bennett.

-I can. It was my father who unearthed it.

-Miss Bennett, I wouldn't advise that. Let me handle this in my own way.

-Of course. That's why I'm here. Had I been in town during that exhibition, I would have tried seizing. it.

-And, ended up like Werner Hoffman?

-I don't know what he tried to do.

-I'm not so sure myself. Anyway, Miss Bennett, where can I get in touch with you?

-At the Waldorf. I'm staying there for a few days with my father. I'd like for you to meet him. He can tell you so much more about the urn and the Sumerians than I can.

Edward got to his feet.

-I'll be taking you up on that.

-Please do. I'll look forward to it. Good day.

-Good day, Miss Bennett.

Ashton Bennett walked into her father's suite at the Waldorf Astoria. She sat down in the armchair directly across from him.

-Well, Ashton, how did your visit with Mr. Mendez go?

-It went well. I told him everything that you instructed me to say. It was a great deal of information for him to think about.

-And, what information did he impart to you?

Ashton smiled and removed her gloves.

-Probably more than he intended.

-I'm listening.

-Marlena Lake does have the urn.

-My suspicions have been confirmed. She is an occultist and must be aware of the dangers.

-Mr. Mendez will speak to her. I'm certain that they're close associates.

-More fool he. Marlena Lake has quite a reputation for ruthlessness and cunning. I wonder what she intends to do with the urn.

-Why not arrange a meeting, father?

-A capital idea, Ashton.

-After all, you do have the original casing that the urn was found in.

-Use that as a bargaining chip, eh? It might work.

-Is the urn your actual objective, father?

-That was a rhetorical question. No. It is not. Luring Edward Mendez to Egypt is the goal. He was there three years ago, but I was unable to contact him.

-Why?

-Mr. Mendez has an affinity with the occult world and yet he remains detached from it and that is all to the good and to his benefit.

-But, what do your need him for? I don't understand.

-As a portal to a future that never will be. Mr. Mendez made a trip into the future and has returned...an experience that he is unaware of...at least, consciously. I, dear daughter, want to know what he saw and experienced.

NINETEEN

MARCO MORALES drove straight to Edward Mendez's office.

-Good work, man. So Prentiss and Cooper are walking hand in hand in this little macabre affair. I wonder...

Marco smiled and pointed a finger at the P. I.

-I know what you wonder, Eddie. Did they murder Cooper's parents. I think they did. It sure sounded like it.

-That makes two of us. But, proof, Marco? That's next to impossible without a confession.

-So, they kill Cooper's parents and wait out the inheritance: a few years – like fifteen -- versus fifty. But, the two girls were with them all the time in the woods..so how the hell did they pull it off?

-Were the girls with them all the time? Kids can be influenced and talked into believing things...things taken out of context or that never even happened.

-So, eliminate them just in case they start remembering what actually took place.

-And, Prentiss might have confided in Miss Matthews.

-Big mistake if he did. Keep your crimes to yourself.

Edward lit up.

-It all makes sense now. Prentiss thought that Lorraine might have blabbed to me. Picking me up was her death warrant; same with April

Marco sat back in his chair.

-So, Eddie, now what? We just sit back and watch them collect?

-Not if I can help it. I got my P. I. gut instinct telling me that those two are gonna' cross swords. One of them is going to want more that the other.

-Which one?

-My money's on Cooper.

-Fair enough, man. I'll take Prentiss.

-The will's being read the day after tomorrow, isn't it? I wonder when they'll start dueling.

Marco took out a piece of gum.

-And, who's gonna' get the death blow?

-Hey, Marco, you up to a return trip to Jersey?

-Like, when, man?

-Like, right now?

-Susan, Professor Bernard Bennett and his daughter are coming for cocktails and dinner tonight.

-Professor Bennett, himself? I've read his articles and his book on ancient Mesopotamia. They're extremely well written.

-Yes. I agree. We should have a great deal to talk about.

-But, why now, mother?

-Rather obvious, that; the Sumerian urn. Professor Bennett wants to see it. He didn't say as much, but I assume that's his reason for phoning. We met briefly in Egypt.

Irene walked in.

-I couldn't help but overhear. Professor Bennett will be here this evening? May I join your party?

-Of course, dear. With your knowledge of science and the Professor's of archaeology, it should be a fascinating evening.

-Mother? Let's invite Edward.

-Will you call him for me, dear? I've things to arrange for tonight.

-I'll call him right now.

-Why not go into my study.

-I was going to.

Susan left the room.

-Irene, tonight I will share my Sumerian urn with Professor Bennett. Have you made your own examination of it?

-I have. It's made of an alloy that appears to be similar to clay. But, I can assure you that it's not clay. And, if I didn't know any better, I would guess that it's a transmitter of sorts.

-Pray, continue.

-I would like to put it under an x-ray to get a good look at its interior.

-Perhaps, Professor Bennett may help us with that.

-How did he find out about the urn, Marlena?

-He has contacts within his field, but I suspect that he knows a great deal more about the urn than any of us. I simply must find out what he does know.

Susan came back into the living room.

-Edward will be coming.

-Good And, let's hope he doesn't bring that ice skater with him.

Marco Morales had been promoted to Detective. He was proud of that promotion. It meant advancement, recognition from his fellow officers and some extra money in his pay check.

Detective Morales had made a U-turn on his way back to New Jersey and was once again sitting in his car opposite Tom Cooper's house. The detective was tired but alert. Two people were in that house. Marco could see their silhouettes by the bay window. The shorter of the two silhouettes was standing still...cowering. The taller of the two was quite demonstrative in his hand and arm gestures. The taller one was Gordon Prentiss. In a split second gesture, he struck down Tom

Cooper...or so it seemed. But, that was enough for Detective Morales. He got out of his car and ran across the street. He banged on the front door. And, to his surprise, the door was opened by Gordon Prentiss.

-Yes? What is it?

-Has someone been injured?

-No.

-I saw what looked like a scuffle.

-There was no scuffle.

-I'm Detective Marco Morales. May I come in for a few seconds?

Before answering, Gordon Prentiss glanced toward the living room.

-Sure, Detective. Come on in.

Marco was led to the living room where Tom Cooper was lowering himself on to the sofa. He looked shaken.

-Mr. Cooper-

-How do you know his name?

Marco ignored Prentiss' query.

-Mr. Cooper, are you hurt?

Without looking up, Cooper answered.

-No. I'm fine.

-Hey, Detective, satisfied?

-I'll have to take Mr. Cooper's word about his health.

-No reason why you shouldn't.

-I'm okay.

-You have Edward Mendez's number. If you need any help at any time, call.

-I thought you were on your way out.

-Just watch your step, buddy...or should I say Mr. Gordon Prentiss...or should I say Mr. Tom Cooper? Take your pick.

-Beat it, cop!

-Must've hit a nerve. I'll be seeing you.

Marco walked out and Prentiss slammed the door after the detective.

-Nathalie? We've been invited to a dinner party of sorts.

-A dinner party? Where, Manuel?

-Tonight, at Marlena Lake's townhouse. Cocktails at seven.

-But, when did this occur?

-Earlier this afternoon. I took the liberty of accepting. It will bring me so much closer to the coveted urn.

-How very convenient.

-Yes. Fate seems to be on our side.

-For the moment. But one mustn't be misled by it.

-Nor should one ignore it.

-Did Miss Lake confide her guest list to you?

-I don't think so. That woman likes to surround herself with learned and interesting people. My son will be there, I'm sure.

-With Yolanda, no doubt.

-Of course. Marlena's daughter, Susan, will be there as usual. She's never anywhere else it seems. A scientist by the name of Miss Irene Wong will attend. Let's see...who else? Lt. William Donovan who is rumored to be promoted to Captain. And, Alexandra Raymond will accompany the Lieutenant; an undercover policewoman of sorts.

-Why in the world invite the police?

-To safeguard the urn, most likely. And, Professor Bernard Bennett and his daughter, Aston, will be coming. Now, there's a man I'd like to meet.

-As you said, an interesting assortment of people. Tell me, Manuel is it a black tie affair?

-I don't think so or Marlena would have mentioned it.

-And, the purpose of this dinner party?

-I know *my* purpose.

-Yes?

-To steal that Sumerian urn.

-Now, that you mention theft, what of Mr. Roger Lee?

-My manservant contacted him. He's awaiting my instructions.

-Can this man be trusted?

-No. He is not to be trusted. But, the lure of money is a lure that Mr. Lee cannot resist. I suffer from the same weakness.

Edward Mendez, P. I. was choosing an appropriate tie for Marlena Lake's dinner party. A solid, navy blue tie would do. It went with his dark blue, custom made suite. And, a white collar shirt would contrast well.

He was going to pick up Yolanda at her place in midtown Manhattan. He was almost ready to leave when someone knocked on his bedroom door.

-Come on in. I'm decent.

Nella walked in.

-Edward, all set for tonight's dinner party?

-I'm just about dressed, if that's what you mean.

-It isn't.

-Thought so. So, dear sister, what exactly do you mean?

-Marlena Lake, if I'm not mistaken, doesn't give casual dinner parties. What is she up to?

-She's up to something. I can guarantee you that.

-It must be the Sumerian urn.

-Nella? Want to come along with me and Yoli? I'm sure she wouldn't mind.

-If I'd been invited, I would.

-I'm sure Marlena wouldn't mind, either.

-Thank you for the offer, Edward. I'll wait for you to tell me and Dottie all about it. We're both bursting with curiosity.

-And, Victoria isn't?

-She's more subtle than we are. But, Edward, how does this impact your investigation into the Lorraine Keyes murder? Is there any connection?

-Only one: our father.

-How is that?

-He bankrolled my investigation into Lorraine's murder: a $10,000 bankroll.

-What's his interest?

-To distract my attention from something much more important to him.

-The Sumerian urn.

-Bulls eye. Or...Lorraine Keyes is...or was...involved with that ancient artifact, somehow.

-She was an interior designer.

-Pretended to be one, at any rate.

-She might have had access to ornamental objects or had an excuse to handle artifacts.

Edward put on his suit jacket.

-Nella, I oughta' put you on commission. I think you've got something there. But, I don't think she was killed for that.

-Why was she killed, Edward?

-Because, she was an unwitting witness to a double murder and-

-Please, don't stop.

-And, she and her sister could break an ironclad alibi.

Detective Marco Morales left Jersey City. He was observed leaving Jersey City by Gordon Prentiss.

-Good. The bastard left...and I can maneuver the body to make it look legit.

Tom Cooper looked as if her were sitting comfortably on his sofa. He was sitting, all right, but he was dead...dead of a bullet wound to the head. The suicide note was on the end table. The bullet had been fired as

soon as Det. Morales was safely out of ear shot. The neighbors would think it was a car backfiring.

-The suicide note and Tom's will...that's all I really need. Now, to call the police. And, to think that Det. Morales gave the perfect excuse for Tom's suicide. The poor boy got scared. He thought that the cops were on to him, so he took the coward's way out. After all, he murdered his parents and guilt never goes away. It'll explain his hermit-like existence and why he left me everything.

-Why in the world did Marlena Lake invite us to cocktails? We don't exactly fit into her circle of friends.

-Police protection.

-Protection from whom, Bill?

-We'll have to work the room to find out. And, we'll give it one helluva' shot.

-I can't wait to see who else she's invited.

-It'll be an interesting crowd.

-I wonder if we'll get to see the infamous urn.

-I'm guessing that's what this is all about, Alex.

-Bill, I've got a real uneasy feeling about that ancient vase. It almost-

-Almost?

-Scares me. I had a good look at it at the museum that night. It's like a time bomb ready to go off in one's face. Look what it did to Werner Hoffman.

-Made mashed potatoes out of his brain. But, he was up to something.

-Whatever it was, it backfired.

Lt. Donovan looked hard at Alexandra Raymond.

-Alex, you're right. You are so friggin' right.

-What did I say?

-That Werner Hoffman was a self serving bastard. He intended to use that vase against us; against anyone in that room in order to make off with it.

-Oh, Bill, I think you're right. He must've thought that by rotating the urn, he wouldn't be affected by it.

-So much for the bastard being some innocent by-stander.

-And, now Marlena Lake's got it back.

-And, she's no fool. That must be the reason for this little get together tonight. She's looking for information, Alex.

-And, protection. That's where we come in. Oh, by the way, Bill, you're looking very handsome.

TWENTY

THE DINNER table was all set. The food was in the kitchen ready to be served at a moment's notice. A chef and waiter had been hired for the occasion.

Meanwhile, in the living room, Marlena Lake was enjoying a cocktail with her daughter, Susan.

-But, where is Miss Wong?

-Last minute primping, mother. She'll be down in a minute or two.

-The first of the guests should be arriving shortly.

-Mother? Dare I ask why you're holding this little dinner party?

-To obtain information, especially from a Mr. Manuel Mendez.

-What can Mr. Mendez possibly tell you that you don't already know?

-He is an occultist and an Adept. He can tell me how to properly handle the urn.

-You are determined to use it.

-Yes.

-To what end, mother?

-Well put, dear. It will serve as a link to the past as well as a connection to that ancient race of aliens.

-How? I really don't understand.

-Vibration is pressure and pressure is what holds the universe in place.

Susan shook her head. It wasn't too often that she didn't understand one of her mother's schemes, but this time the young woman was baffled.

The doorbell rang.

-Would you answer that, Susan?

Susan went to the front door. Two couples were waiting just outside.

-Edward and Yolanda. When did you get back in town, Yolanda?

-Just the other day. How are you, Susan?

-I'm fine. Please, come in. Mother's in the living room.

Susan looked to the other couple: Lt. Donovan and Alexandra Raymond.

-Lt. Donovan and Miss Raymond. Please, come in.

In another moment, the six people were gathered in Marlena's living room. Susan was tending the drinks table. Irene Wong finally came down the flight of stairs. She looked stunning in her midnight blue Mandarin dress.

-I apologize for being late. It's bad manners.

-Not at all, dear. I believe you know everyone here.

-Of course.

Miss Wong gravitated toward Edward and Yolanda. Marlena, who was sitting in one of the armchairs, asked everyone to have a seat. She started in on Yolanda. Yolanda was expecting this.

-Dear Yolanda, whatever brings you back to New York? I thought we had lost you to the wilds of the Amazon.

Yolanda smiled sweetly.

-I'm sitting next to that reason. I made a mistake in leaving. I should have known better.

The young woman turned to Edward.

-And, I will never make that mistake, again.

She put her hand through Edward's arm. Marlena didn't attempt to hide her smirk.

-How very touching. One would say, romantic.

Alex Raymond offered interference for Yolanda. A few months ago, she wouldn't, but her affections had shifted to the man sitting beside her: Lt. Donovan.

-Yolanda? Have you given up skating or have you turned professional?

-I wouldn't mind doing local tours, but nothing too far from home and Edward.

Miss Wong joined the conversation.

-I so admire athleticism. I get so little chance at physical sports. I've seen your resume, Miss Estravades. I was quite impressed with your accomplishments.

-Thank you, Miss Wong. That's very kind of you.

-Not at all. The facts speak for themselves.

Marlena turned her attention to Edward and Lt. Donovan.

-Edward? What news of the Lorraine Keyes case? Lieutenant? Anything on your end to report? I must admit that the case interests me.

Edward answered first.

-Actually, Marlena, plenty. We have a prime suspect.

-And, of course, the evidence to back it up?

Lt. Donovan answered her.

-Not yet. But, there is a witness...a key witness who we're about to put under police protection.

-Outstanding, gentlemen. You must let me know how it all turns out.

The doorbell rang and Susan went to answer it. When the young girl opened the door, she barely suppressed a gasp. Professor Bernard Bennett and Ashton Bennett were standing there. Susan was taken aback with Ashton Bennett's beauty...a classic and striking beauty. She couldn't help thinking how Yolanda and Irene would take to Miss Bennett.

But, in fact, Susan looked long and hard at Professor Bernard Bennett. She had not expected to see such an old man as he. The professor stood tall and erect, but his face was hard, pale and lined with wrinkles. His eyes were dark...almost black holes that Susan found quite disconcerting. His hands...his hands had the sheen of white marble. Susan had to catch her breath a second time. This man looked eerily familiar to her.

-Please, forgive me. Please...come in. I'm Susan Broder. I'm Marlena's daughter.

Miss Bennett acknowledged the greeting.

-Pleased to meet you, Miss Broder. Your mother's reputation precedes her.

-Yes, Miss Broder. Good evening. I'm quite anxious to meet Miss Lake. Our paths nearly crossed in Egypt several years ago. Will you show us in?

-Of course.

Professor Bennett and Ashton followed Susan into the living room. Everyone there looked up as they came in... all conversations stopped abruptly. Susan broke the silence by way of introductions. And, still she wondered where she had seen Professor Bennett before. It was recently-

To herself.

-He was the man looking at me through the window the other night. It wasn't Werner Hoffman after all. It was Professor Bennett.

This revelation sent shivers up and down Susan's spine. For the moment, she kept this information to herself.

Yolanda smiled graciously at Miss Bennett. The Spanish beauty appreciated Miss Bennett's Nordic beauty, but did not feel threatened by it. Ashton Bennett wasn't Edward's type.

Irene liked the girl because she struck her as being intelligent and worldly. She did not really care for her "cold" beauty, though. A man might find warmth in it, but she did not.

Everyone in the room was taken aback by Professor Bennett's appearance. However, they had the good manners not to make it obvious. Edward lit a cigarette hoping to disguise his scrutiny of the professor. Lt. Donovan did the same thing, while Alex Raymond took out her compact for a minor "repair" job.

Susan got the new arrivals their drinks. And, Professor Bennett got straight to the heart of the matter. He addressed Marlena.

-Miss Lake, might I at one point in the evening view your Sumerian urn? I am most anxious to see it. I hope you don't mind my directness.

-Of course not, Professor Bennett. I would appreciate your knowledge of Sumerian culture and in particular the origin of that race which is shrouded in mystery and speculation.

-I have my own theories on it.

-I'm eager to hear them.

Alex Raymond who had put away her compact asked her question.

-Professor Bennett? Did the Sumerians fashion that deadly urn?

-One would assume so in light of no contradictory evidence. Why do you ask, Miss Raymond?

-I've got this feeling that another race pre-dated the Sumerians...an even more advanced race..and they were the ones who manufactured it.

-Manufacture, Miss Raymond? How interesting that you should use that particular word.

Susan joined in the conversation.

-I wonder where that other race came from?

Edward answered her.

-The Anunanki: the gods who descended from heaven or from another planet or from someplace.

Professor Bennett was impressed with the P. I's answer.

-Mr. Mendez, you state from "heaven" that they descended to the Earth.

The P. I. grinned.

-Well, from another planet.

-Within this solar system? Is that your meaning?

-Why not? How much do we really know about our own solar system?

Professor Bennett nodded his approval.

-Not all that much. We've yet to reach our own moon.

Yolanda was about to speak, but Lt. Donovan jumped in.

-These Anunanki, Professor, whatever happened to them? Did they go back where they came from...wherever that is?

-Yes and no, Lieutenant. Perhaps, most left and, perhaps, some stayed to found the city of Sumer.

-But, getting back to the urn; is it a weapon of some sort?

Professor Bennett evaded the Lieutenant's question.

-A device that was used for mining purposes among other purposes.

-Like splitting bedrock?

-Or even splitting the core of a planet. But, one can only guess at this point, though.

Now, Yolanda joined in.

-My God, Professor Bennett, what are you telling us? Is this some kind of a doomsday weapon?

Before he could answer, Yolanda continued.

-This urn should be destroyed. No one is safe if what you are telling us is true.

Professor Bennett was about to speak when a voice from the living room doorway cut him off.

-Destroy a priceless work of scientific genius? I wouldn't hear of it, Miss Estravades.

Edward's back was to that voice, but he had no trouble recognizing it. He stood up and turned to face it.

-Father.

-Edward, you're looking well.

Manuel Mendez turned to Marlena.

-My apologies for my late arrival. Nathalie and I were unavoidably detained.

Susan spoke up.

-Mr. Mendez? Miss Montaigne? May I offer you a drink?

-Scotch for me. Nathalie? What are you having?

-Scotch and water, cherie.

Neither person made a move to sit down.

-Miss Lake? Have you exhibited the urn to your assembled guests, yet?

-I was waiting for your arrival, Mr. Mendez. As a fellow occultist, I place a great value on your knowledge.

-Good. As you should.

Susan handed Mr. Mendez his drink.

-Thank you. Miss Lake? The urn?

It was in the tone of an order and not a request.

Marlena looked about the room and asked her guests a general question.

-Shall I exhibit the urn before we sit down to dinner? Would anyone object?

No one objected.

-Very well. Susan, would you fetch it for mother, dear?

-Of course.

-It's in the wall safe. You know the combination. You've conquered your fear of it.

Susan left the room not quite agreeing with her mother's last statement. Marlena addressed Manuel Mendez.

-Mr. Mendez, I don't appreciate being ordered about in my own home.

-If my tone offended you, Miss Lake, I apologize. But, I am anxious to see this ancient marvel.

-Why?

That was Miss Raymond asking that question.

-Because I require it, young lady.

-That's not an answer.

-It is my answer for now. Whether you like it or not is of no concern to me.

Edward spoke in Alex's defense.

-Alex only asked you a civil question. And, I'm not fond of evasiveness, father. What the hell is your game here? What do you want? Is that direct enough for you?

Manuel Mendez glared at his son.

-The urn.

-It's not yours.

Now, it was Marlena's turn.

-I've no intention of giving it up to you or to anyone, Mr. Mendez.

-You may change your mind.

-Highly unlikely.

Yolanda spoke to Manuel Mendez.

-What do you plan on doing with it, Mr. Mendez?

-That is no concern of yours, young lady.

Professor Bennett spoke.

-It is a dangerous artifact, sir. Are you are aware of its full potential?

-I am. It can shatter worlds as it once did.

-When was this?

Ashton Bennett spoke.

-Was it the cause of the asteroid belt near Mars?

-Yes. In a cataclysmic war that preceded mankind.

-I agree with Miss Estravades. If what you say is true, it should be destroyed.

Manuel Mendez spoke.

-Or sent back to its original owners.

-How on earth would you do that and why?

-The urn would do it for me, Miss Bennett.

Edward, who was still standing and facing his father, spoke.

-How? Give me a concrete answer.

-Perhaps, Edward, I don't care to give you an answer.

The P. I. grinned.

-You like playing the mystery man, don't you, father?

Lt. Donovan was about to join in when Susan came back into the room carrying the urn.

-Susan, bring the urn to mother, please.

-May I examine it first?

-No, Mr. Mendez, you may not.

-And, if I insist, Miss Lake?

-Do not press me on this matter, Mr. Mendez, or I will have to ask you to leave.

Manuel Mendez was no longer addressing Marlena.

-Miss Broder, I will take that urn.

Before Susan could respond, Edward came between her and his father.

-You're not thinking of walking out of here with that urn, are you?

-Yes, young man, that is exactly what I intend to do.

-Then, you'll have to walk through me.

-Keep out of this, Edward.

-Make me.

Manuel Mendez was beside himself with rage.

-Why you arrogant, ungrateful bastard! How *dare* you speak to me in that manner?

-Thought that you bought me off for ten grand, huh?

-Frankly, yes. You did take the money.

-It was for Lorraine Keyes that I took it.

-A case that you will never solve.

-Don't make bet on it. I've been circling around a couple of suspects.

-You're wasting my time.

Manuel Mendez turned to Susan who was still holding on to the urn.

-I'll take that urn, young lady.

Lt. Donovan stood up along with Alex Raymond.

-Miss Broder, give that urn to your mother. Mr. Mendez is leaving without it.

Susan handed the urn to her mother.

Manuel Mendez reached into his jacket and and took out a pistol.

-It has come to this. Lieutenant? Miss Raymond? Edward? Do not attempt to draw your weapons. I have no compunction in killing any of you unless you force my hand.

Marlena, who always carried her handbag with her even in her own house, now reached into it. She took out her handgun, but Manuel caught her in the act.

-Careful, Miss Lake.

Miss Bennett spoke.

-You can't possibly get away with this, Mr. Mendez. Even if you take the urn, the police will hunt you down. It can't possibly be worth it to you.

-It is worth it, my dear.

Professor Bennett spoke, pointing his now empty glass at Manuel Mendez.

-Please, Mr. Mendez, as men of the world, put that gun away. Let us all work together and pool our resources toward understanding this urn. Violence, tonight, is not necessary.

Marlena interjected. She had put away her gun and was now firmly holding on to the urn with both hands.

-My object-

Manuel Mendez cut her off. He was growing more and more impatient.

-You are a fool, Miss Lake, if you actually believe that. It belongs to the race who created it and to no one else.

Edward almost laughed.

-Bulls eye. Meaning it doesn't belong to you, father. And, if you take it by force, you won't get ten feet from this house.

Miss Wong spoke and did not mince her words.

-You think that you know how to use this weapon, don't you? That's why you want it: it will give you power. You are a megalomaniac, Mr. Mendez.

-You know too much, Miss Wong. And, I am not interested in your opinion.

-Your type is always easy to spot.

Yolanda spoke to Marlena.

-Just give it to him. Edward will hunt him down.

Marlena had a nasty smile on her face.

-Very well, Mr. Mendez...here...catch!

-Mother, don't!

Manuel Mendez didn't drop his gun. Instead, he made a grab for the urn that had just been flung at him. He missed it. Nathalie caught it and was flung back against the far wall. She screamed and passed out, dropping the urn to the floor. It landed undamaged on the thick pile carpet. But, then, a tremor shook the town-house. Those who were standing were knocked to the floor. Windows shattered, brick-a-brac toppled form shelves and every light bulb in the house burst.

Manuel Mendez had been prepared for this and was the first to get to his feet. He grabbed the urn and made for the front door. Edward and Lt. Donovan got up, but the Lieutenant's attention was drawn to Miss Raymond who had fallen against an end table. He helped her up.

Edward gave chase to his father but the latter who had just flung open the front door turned about and took a shot at his son, but barely grazed him on the fore-head. It stunned Edward, giving his father a chance to reach his car and escape. He left a dazed Nathalie Mon-taigne behind. Despite the blood running into his eyes,

Edward followed his father, firing shots at the rear view window. It shattered, but the car did not slow down.

Lt. Donovan came up from behind, aimed and fired at the right rear tire.

-Damn it!

The Lieutenant noticed Edward's wound.

-Mendez, are you okay?

-Just bleeding like a stuck pig.

-Let's get you inside. We'll call the medics.

-No. I'll be okay. But, we should go after him.

-I'll put out an A.P.B. I got the license plate number and car make. We'll get the bastard.

The two men went back inside Marlena's townhouse. People were just recovering their senses. Alex Raymond was helping Nathalie Montaigne get to her feet. The Frenchwoman was dazed but otherwise unharmed. Lt. Donovan approached her.

-Did you know what Manuel Mendez was up to?

Natalie Montaigne had prepared a litany of lies just in case Manuel Mendez failed in his attempt to steal urn or if she were somehow caught.

-No. Mon Dieu! I swear by all the saints that I did not know. I knew that he wanted the urn and was prepared to offer money but...this...he could have killed us all!

-Alex, stay with Miss Montaigne. I'm gonna' call this in.

Alex Raymond continued where Lt. Donovan had left off.

-Where is Mr. Mendez headed? You must know that much.

-I do not. Surely, not back to Miranda Drake's place. But-

-Yes? He'd have enough nerve to go back there, wouldn't he?

-He would, cherie. He is far too clever. Put nothing past him.

-And, brazen. Don't leave that out.

Lt. Donovan was now on the phone to the 86th Precinct. Edward was checking on everyone in the living room. The P. I. was more than upset with Marlena, who seemed surprisingly unphased by it all.

-Marlena, you could have killed us all. You do know that.

-Dear boy, a mere toss of a few feet? I thought it would stun your father. Admittedly, I miscalculated.

-I'll say! I think every piece of glass in the place is shattered...light bulbs included.

He turned to Yolanda.

-Baby, you okay?

-Just a little shaken.

-I want you to spend the night here. Marlena, can you put up Yoli for the night?

-Of course.

-Good. 'Cause I'm gonna be tracking down Mr. Manuel Mendez. Professor Bennett? Miss Bennett? How are you two holding up?

Professor Bennett answered.

-We're fine, Mr. Mendez. Thank you. But, you must retrieve that urn at all costs.

-My father is right, Mr. Mendez. We're all in danger now. The entire city is in danger. And- your forehead! You're bleeding.

Susan came over.

-Edward, let's get you cleaned up. Come on. It's straight to the medicine cabinet and no arguments.

Edward smiled.

-You convinced me.

Susan led the P. I. up to the second floor bathroom and bandaged his grazed forehead.

-Edward, any idea where your dad might be headed.

-Well, as soon as you finish with me, I'm heading into Brooklyn Heights. Gotta' check out the obvious.

-That makes sense. And, if he's not there?

-My mom's place.

Susan smiled.

-And, then?

-I think a graveyard where my family mausoleum is.

-Why in the world would you go there?

-He's an occultist, Susan. He knows all the tricks of that dark trade. And, I wouldn't put anything past him -- not after tonight.

Alex Raymond called from downstairs.

-Edward? Phone call for you. It's Marco.

-Susan, are we finished?

-Just about.

-Thanks. You're a regular Clara Barton.

-I read that book.

Edward practically ran down the flight of stairs. Alex was waiting for him at the bottom landing.

-Take it easy, there. Marco won't hang up.

-Thanks, Alex.

Edward went into the living room and picked up the receiver.

-Marco? It's Edward. What's up?

-You sitting down?

-No. But, I'm leaning against a wall.

-Tom Cooper blew his brains out not two hours ago.

-A suicide?

-Looks that way, sort of.

-You mean it could be a homicide?

-I'd like to talk to you about that in person.

-You want to come over to Marlena's by foot? I've got my car and I'll be tracking down a relative of mine. I could use the company.

-You bet. Lt. Donovan filled me in. Give me about ten minutes.

Irene approached Edward. She was holding her high heels in her hand.

-Irene, are you okay? Didn't meant to ignore you.

-I understand. And, I'm uninjured. I was sitting down at the time, but the very air around me shifted as if it were solid matter. That urn, Edward, you must retrieve it at all costs before it causes irreparable damage.

And, eleven minutes later, Edward was heading into Brooklyn with Marco in the front passenger seat. The ride across the Brooklyn Bridge was pleasant enough under the circumstances.

-So, Marco, what else did your contact in Jersey have to say? And, by the way, you've got more contacts than I can shake a stick at.

Marco laughed at the left-handed compliment.

-The original Mr. Tom Cooper wasn't alone.

-Why am I not surprised?

-Gordon Prentiss just happened to be with him.

-Egging him on to blow his brains out.

-That's my guess, too. So, now who inherits?

-That's the million dollar question. A lot of red tape might be involved. Mr. Prentiss just might have to wait for his blood money as the newly christened Tom Cooper.

-What some people won't do for money.

-*That* you can say again.

-So, Eddie, to change the subject, your father took off with that Sumerian urn.

Edward forced a smile.

-After Marlena flung it at him.

-But, why turn himself into a wanted man? He'll be hunted down now and looking over his shoulder.

-He'll go underground. He's used to that. And, he's got the money for it...thanks to Miranda Drake.

-But, what does he want with the damned urn?

-To practice some of his hocus-pocus with it. Or to blackmail person or persons with it? Take your pick. As Miss Wong pointed out, my father's a megalomaniac. He's vain, selfish and an egotist.

-He sounds pretty dangerous.

-He is. I don't underestimate him not for one damned second. Here's that turn-off. We're almost there.

And, in another couple of minutes, Edward was parked in front of the late Miranda Drake's mansion. The front door was locked, so Edward and Marco forced it open. They entered the foyer and heard footsteps coming toward them. Both men drew their guns. Marco turned to Edward.

-Hey, man, it can't be your dad, can it?

It wasn't. It was Manuel Mendez's manservant.

-Good God! What is it? What do you want?

-I'm Edward Mendez. We've met. And, this is Det. Marco Morales.

-Oh, but-

-Is your Master at home?

-No. He left earlier this evening with Miss Montaigne.

-He hasn't returned?

-Why, no. At least...

-Mind if we have a look around?

-I'm sure that your father wouldn't mind.

-Good. We won't disturb anything, will we, Marco?

-We'll be real careful.

This sarcasm wasn't lost on the manservant.

After about twenty minutes of looking into every room and closet, the two men went back to the foyer where Manuel Mendez's manservant was patiently waiting for them.

-Okay. No sign of my father.

-I'm sure that I would have heard him return.

-Your name?

-Michael, Mr. Mendez.

-Surname?

-Runyon.

-Okay, Mr. Runyon, if my father returns, you're obligated to call the police or call me. Here's my card.

-And, what about Miss Montaigne?

-Same for her.

-As you wish, Mr. Mendez.

-And, Mr. Runyon, You have nothing to worry about. But, the police will be here some time tonight.

-I'll expect them. Mr. Mendez, is your father in some sort of trouble?

-And, of his own making.

TWENTY-ONE

THE NEXT morning, Lt William Donovan received a phone call from Manuel Mendez.

The next morning, Edward Mendez, P. I. received a phone call from Gordon Prentiss.

-Lt. Donovan speaking.

-Lt. Donovan, Manuel Mendez.

-Yes, Mr. Mendez?

-Your tone of voice speaks of caution.

-What do your want? Why the phone call; to give yourself up?

-No. To make clear my demands.

Lt. Donovan frantically waved to his officer who was standing outside his office to have this phone call traced.

-What are these demands?

-To have one hundred million dollars delivered by my son, Edward, to the address that I will specify only to him.

-You're insane, pal. And, just why should we deliver *anything* to you?

-After I hang up, a demonstration will take place. Oh, nothing fatal or too drastic...just a reminder that you are at my mercy.

-Sorry, pal. No dice. Turn yourself in...no real damage has been done.

-But, the dice will be rolled and soon. Now, I will hang up and within minutes an abandoned factory in the heart of Jersey City will be reduced to powder.

-Where in Jersey City? Will any civilians be in danger?

-Yes. But, unfortunately, innocent bystanders are expendable. And, to answer your first question: the abandoned Silver Cup factory on Palmetto St. and Wilson Ave. If you're so concerned about innocent bystanders, have the area cleared within a half mile radius.

-A bomb's set to go off?

-Nothing as crude as a bomb. Get the money by this evening and deliver it to Edward Mendez.

-That's impossible-

-Good day, Lieutenant.

Manuel Mendez hung up. The officer outside his office came running in.

-Couldn't trace it, Lieutenant. At least, we couldn't pinpoint it, but it's somewhere in the Jersey City area.

-Get Marco Morales up here.

-Right away.

The officer went in search of Det. Morales. Lt. Donovan dialed Edward Mendez's office. The line was busy.

-Damn it! Damn it! *Damn it*!

Edward Mendez was speaking to Gordon Prentiss.

-Hi, Mr. Mendez. It's Tom Cooper. By the way, Tom Cooper's dead. Suicide. I was there. I saw it. Poor devil...must have been a guilty conscience. Or maybe your pal, Morales, pushed him over the edge.

-You pushed him over the edge. You took his name and now you're taking over his life. Tell me something, did you kill his parents? You can tell me.

-Tom Cooper killed his parents.

-Meaning?

-Meaning, you're out of your mind if you think I'll answer that question.

-Hey, Gordon?

-Tom's the name.

-Gordon, you already answered it.

-Just get the hell off my back. Tom's dead and you've got nothing on me.

-Tom's dead. April and Lorraine are dead.

-And, don't forget about Miss Matthews.

-Talk about shooting yourself in the foot.

-I read the obituaries every day. Keeps me updated.

-It wasn't in the obituaries.

-It had to be.

-It wasn't. We made certain of that.

The line went dead.

Dottie poked her head in Edward's office.

-Eddie, Lt. Donovan's on the line and he sounds pretty worked up.

-So am I. Put him through, Dottie.

-Sure thing.

Lt. Donovan's call was transferred.

-Hey, Lieutenant, I got news for you.

-If you don't mind, Mendez, I'll go first. And, it ain't good news.

-I'm ready when you are.

Lt. Donovan relayed Manuel Mendez's message.

-My old man's gone off his rocker.

-How's he gonna' blow up that warehouse?

-With that damned Sumerian urn. You know, the urn from hell. Just how he's gonna' trigger it off for a specific location....that, I don' know.

-We're clearing the area, but it'll take time. And, he said that we don't have any time.

-My old man's nothing but a cold blooded murderer.

The explosion was not an explosion. The building vibrated as if it were made of jelly. The air around the warehouse turned a vaporous white that shimmered. The sound was deafening. The police who were clearing the area fell to the ground in a vain attempt to cover their ears. People screamed in agony and passed out...many permanently brain damaged or dead.

The three story warehouse trembled, but didn't topple. It disintegrated as if made of sand. It collapsed in upon itself...even its steel girders that remained upright crumbled like so much dust at the touch of a finger.

The demonstration was complete.

-Mr. Mendez, even the steel beams are crumbling.

Edward Mendez stood next to Lt. Donovan. In front of them was an immense hill of powder and debris that had once been a warehouse. The P. I. forced the words from his throat.

-I still can't believe that my father would do this. He's ruthless and cunning, but to murder innocent people in an obscure location just doesn't make sense.

-What doesn't make sense?

-Why here in Jersey City? It's just not his style. If he'd targeted some place in Manhattan; that I could understand.

-We'd better get back to my office. His call's gonna be coming through and we've got a pile of money to collect and hand over. And, how in the hell we're gonna' do it, I don't know.

-I'll meet you back there. I want to make a couple of stops.

Edward Mendez walked into Nathalie Montaigne's hospital room. The Frenchwoman was sitting up in bed as if expecting the P. I.

-Edward, cherie. You have come to visit Nathalie. How very kind of you.

-Technically, yes. But, I've got a couple of questions for you, if you're up to it.

-Please. It will relieve the boredom.

-Will you be getting out soon?

-I wanted to leave today, but the doctor insisted on at least a twenty-four hour observation. I do want to get back to the bookshop.

-Did my father, Nathalie-

-You call me by my first name. Splendid.

-And, you can call me Edward.

-Lovely. We are friends then?

-Nathalie, did my father ever mention anything about a demonstration of power or anything about ransom money?

Nathalie Montaigne decided to tell the truth. It was so much easier to remember the facts as they actually occurred.

-Yes, Edward, he did. You see? A straight forward answer, cherie.

-I appreciate that. Did he confide any details to you? Anything that you remember will help.

-He was toying with the idea of targeting the Chrysler Building.

Edward slapped the wall behind him.

-Yes! That's more his style.

-What do you mean, Edward? What has happened?

The P. I. told her.

-Mon Dieu! He would not do that, Edward. Never. He was careful to mention evacuating the building first. Manuel is no mass murderer even though he would speak cavalierly about such a thing. I can assure you of that. And, some God forsaken spot in New Jersey? I doubt if Manuel has ever even been there. No! His so-called demonstration would be spectacular and memorable without harm to anyone if possible.

Edward agreed. So, why New Jersey? Who could give him an answer?

He kissed Nathalie on the cheek.

-Lt. Donovan, that was my father you spoke to this morning?

-Who else would it be? Had to be him.. Sounded like him.

-But, now that you think of it...

-The Spanish accent was there, but...

-But? I don't want to put words in your mouth.

-But, a little too much of an accent.

-Like someone trying to fake an accent and going overboard on it?

-Could be. Why this doubt, Mendez?

-A factory in New Jersey is not my father's style – not spectacular enough. And, he wouldn't want any fatalities, not if he could help it.

-You think.

-Okay. I'm not one hundred percent on this, but close to it. When he makes that next phone call, I want to be listening in.

-You will be. He didn't say when, but he's probably giving us time to absorb the damage in Jersey.

Forty-five minutes later... Edward stopped off at his office. Dottie was full of questions. The destruction of the warehouse had been heard clear across the river. The P. I. filled his sister in on the details.

-I can't believe he's behind this.

-I'm having the same trouble. But, if he isn't, then who is?

-I don't know. I just don't know.

-But, I should know.

-Well, Mr. P. I.?

-Someone who's familiar with the Jersey City layout.

-A resident?

-Bulls eye.

-Well, give!

-I don't see the connection, but Gordon Prentiss who now calls himself Tom Cooper.

-Sort of makes sense. But, what's his connection with our father? And, how did Prentiss get the urn?

Edward sat down on the chair opposite Dottie.

-I've been thinking real hard on that one.

-And?

-Gordon Prentiss worked for Romo-Ark and I'm convinced that our father has connections with them. And, that would put him in touch with Prentiss.

-And, our father would just let Prentiss have use of the urn from hell? I can't believe it.

-Neither can I. And, I'm really guessing now, but I think Prentiss took it from him and used it.

-So, where's Mr. Manuel Mendez now?

Edward shook his head in the negative.

-Dead, maybe.

-Oh, God!

-Gordon Prentiss is a killer. He's killed at least three people...maybe five, including the Coopers.

-And, six counting our father.

-Our father might not have been so easy to kill. He could be in hiding.

There was a knock on the door and Ginny Gray burst in.

-Okay, Mendez, I want the scoop on the explosion in Jersey.

Once again, Edward related the details as he knew them.

-So, Mendez, where's Prentiss and your dad? We've gotta' find them and fast. So far, thirty seven people are counted as dead and a couple of hundred are deaf...maybe for life.

Edward took out a cigarette and lit up.

Ginny sat down next to him.

-What about that dame, Nathalie Montaigne?

Edward's face lit up.

-Ginny? Dottie? I want you both to pay her a visit, like right now. No. Check that.

He raced into his office and dialed the hospital while Ginny and Dottie raced after him.

-Hello? Put me through to Nathalie Montaigne, please. She's a patient.

He held on to the receiver.

-Yes? Who is calling?

-Nathalie, it's Edward. I've gotta' get straight to the point. Did my father mention where he would operate the Sumerian urn? Not from his place in Brooklyn, surely.

-No. Not there.

-Where, Nathalie? Please, try to remember.

-I'm sorry, cherie. I'm still very much in a daze. It simply won't come.

-Nathalie, if you do remember, call Lt. Donovan at the 86th immediately.

-Of course, Edward. I promise. But, you should also know that your father contacted Roger Lee. Mr. Lee was to be a participant.

-Roger Lee, huh? I don't have time to track that hood down. It'll have to be another day for him.

Edward hung up the phone.

Ginny spoke.

-Who else might know, Eddie?

An idea rang in Edward's brain.

-It's a long shot, but just maybe Henriette Miller could help out.

Ginny got to her feet.

-Well, what are we waiting for. Where is this chick?

-In the Houston library. Dottie, man the phone. I'll be in touch. And, call Donovan and tell him about our friend, Miss Montaigne. Maybe, he can jog her memory. Ginny get in touch with Marlena and shake her down for any details about that God forsaken urn. And, if you want to catch up with me, I'll be paying a visit to Tom Cooper's house in a little while.

TWENTY-TWO

-HENRIETTE.

-Edward, so glad to see you, again. But, what happened in New Jersey? You must tell me.

Edward told her.

-How terrible.

-It could have been a lot worse.

-What will happen now?

-Henriette, when you saw Werner Hoffman that night, where exactly was he headed?

-In the direction of the cemetery in Highland Park.

-Where in the cemetery? Do you have any idea? Mind you, I think I already know.

-I lost sight of him when he crossed the street, but maybe I should have said something at the time.

-Like what?

-An upstairs neighbor of mine is one of the custodians there. He is a very nice man. I told him what I had seen and he said that one of the mausoleums had been broken into. Well, almost- the outer gate was still locked, but it had been tampered with.

Edward leaned against the check-out counter.

-Yes. I just bet I know whose mausoleum it was.

-Whose Edward?

-The Mendez mausoleum.

-Will you go there now?

-I can't think of anything else to do.

-May I go with you?

-It could be dangerous.

-But, we are all in danger. And, I want to help.

Henriette turned to her supervisor who had been listening.

-It's all right, Henriette. Your shift's almost up and I'll cover for you. But, Please be careful. Mr. Mendez? You look after her now.

-I will. Promise.

Thirty minutes later, Edward and Henriette were crossing the street and entering Highland Park cemetery. The sun was just above the horizon and dusk was approaching. The cemetery gate was open.

-But, the sun is so bright and blinding. You can barely look toward the west.

-I'll say. Hey, Henriette, is there a pay phone nearby? I'd like to check in with Lt. Donovan.

-Not in the cemetery, surely. But, over there, across the street, there is a phone booth.

-Good. After we've checked out the mausoleum, I'll give the Lieutenant a buzz.

The two people walked along the perimeter path until-

-There it is.

They left the path and walked left toward the Mendez mausoleum.

-The iron gate's intact.

-But, Edward, it's locked.

The P. I. withdrew a skeleton key from his jacket pocket.

-I'll fix that.

Edward inserted the key into the lock, turned it and it clicked open. He grabbed the handle of the iron door.

-Henriette, stand back.

The door's handle turned easily enough. Edward placed his foot against it and shoved the door open. He crouched down not knowing what to expect.

-I'm quite harmless. You may come in.

Manuel Mendez was sitting on the mausoleum floor. His hands and feet were tied. And, it looked as if he had just loosed the gag that had been around his mouth.

Edward rushed in and untied his father. Henriette came and helped Manuel Mendez to his feet.

-Thank you.

Edward sat his father down on the edge of what had been his coffin.

-Very apropos, wouldn't you say, son?

-In a twisted way. Listen, father, there may not be much time left.

-There isn't. Of course, I know why you're here.

Henriette, who was sitting next to Manuel felt compelled to give some needed advice.

-Edward, your father doesn't look well. Perhaps, we should get him to a hospital?

-Thank you, young lady; but much more than my health is at stake.

He turned to Edward.

-Gordon Prentiss. The story is complex, but it is he who you must stop.

-Where is he? You've gotta' know.

-In Tom Cooper's home. You know where it is.

-I should by now. But, how? How is he doing it?

-Through the black arts that I've taught him.

-For God's sake, why?

-I'll explain later. But, you've no time to lose. He has no regard for human life. I hadn't realized that and I should have. If you can get the urn from him – and that may not be as easy as you think – destroy it by fire...place it into a furnace. And, that fool may have unwittingly transmitted a signal to the Anunanki themselves on their home planet. Pray that he hasn't.

The three people emerged from the mausoleum to be greeted by one of the cemetery's caretakers. Henriette recognized him as her upstairs neighbor.

-Brendan, I'm so glad that you're here. It's all right. Mr. Mendez and his father own this mausoleum.

-Then, it's okay, I guess.

Edward addressed the caretaker.

-Hey, Brendan, we could use your help. My father's not too steady on his feet and should be taken to a hospital right away.

-He doesn't look too good.

-Can you get back to your office and call an ambulance?

-I'll run back, Mr. Mendez.

-Thanks so much.

The P. I. turned his attention to Henriette.

-Henriette, stay here with my father. Okay? I've gotta' run and catch up with Gordon Prentiss.

Before Henriette or Manuel Mendez could say anything, Edward made a b-line out of the mausoleum and ran straight to the telephone booth on the opposite corner of the cemetery. He put in a call to Lt. Donovan.

-Hello, Lieutenant? Bill?

-Mendez? Couldn't get anything out of Miss Montaigne. She either doesn't remember or she's lying.

-It's okay. I've got my old man and he's put me on to Gordon Prentiss.

-Prentiss was behind the warehouse destruction?

-Yep. And, I'm headed to the Cooper house. That's where Prentiss is now. Send me all the back up you can spare.

-Done. But, just how much time do we have before he makes another move?

-Don't know. But, I'm on my way to breaking some speed limit records.

-Where's your father now?

-In Highland Cemetery, but he'll be headed for Wyckoff Hospital soon enough. Henriette Miller's with him.

-Henriette? What the hell is she doing there?

-Never mind. I'll fill you in later.

The P. I. hung up.

In the ambulance, on the way to Wyckoff Hospital...

-Mr. Mendez, lie still.

-Yes. I must conserve my strength. My time may be near at hand and I've much to say.

-I am sure that it can wait.

-Henriette?

-Yes. I am listening.

-You strike me as a very honest and stable young woman. Listen carefully. After my "death," I was forced to go underground. My enemies were too many for my resources to fight. I didn't fear my immediate followers within my own encampment. They were loyal if fearful of me. It was Romo-Ark and their henchmen who I feared. Like Marlena Lake, they too search for ancient artifacts. But, I daresay that Miss Lake is far more clever than they.

-From what I have heard of her, yes. I must agree with you.

-The urn must be destroyed for it is not an urn. Would be that it were something so mundane. It is a part of a mechanism that no living being should possess. By itself, only the art of magic can direct its energy. I trusted Gordon Prentiss and he betrayed me. He seemed a lonely and troubled young man who I mistakenly took pity on. Henriette, pity no stranger.

-Mr. Mendez, we are almost to the hospital.

-I must continue. I instructed Gordon on how to get employment at Romo-Ark. He needed the money and I needed an informant on the inside who I could trust. And, he did his part. He kept me informed to the extent that I could continuously emerge from my underground exile. I made more contacts: Mr. Roger Lee, Miss Marlena Lake and even Miranda Drake who I shamelessly used.

-We are arriving at the hospital.

-Henriette, my Last Will and Testament is in the wall safe at Miss Drake's former residence. Edward will inherit everything. The combination-

-Mr. Mendez, are you-

The ambulance attendants wheeled Manuel Mendez into the emergency room. He'd gone into cardiac arrest. The attending physician failed to revive him.

Edward Mendez, P. I. pulled right up to the late Tom Cooper's house. He got out of his DeSoto, ran to the front door and didn't bother to knock. He kicked open the door with his gun drawn. The first floor was dark and there was not sign of anyone, but he knew where to go: to the basement. He kicked open that door and bounded down the wood plank steps. When he reached the bottom, he stopped and listened.

-Back here, Mr. P. I. You don't have much time, but I've got plenty.

Gun draw, Edward walked to the back of the cellar. Gordon Prentiss was sitting cross legged on the cement floor and the urn was placed directly in front of him.

-Okay, Mr. Gordon Prentiss, hand over the urn.

-Make me. Because, you'll have to kill me to get your stinking hands on it.

-Don't force my hand, pal. If it means saving lives, yours is a pretty small price to pay.

-Whaddya' know? You're a murderer like me. I like that.

-You're a cold-blooded bastard with no regard for life. You kill and don't give a damn.

-I killed Lorraine Keyes and her sister...well, Jack Dana did that last one for me. Don't try and find him, you won't.

-Tell me what I don't know, creep.

-I even killed that bleeding heart, Miss Matthews. And, April's upstairs neighbor...that was real easy...just one good shove off the train platform. Too bad April didn't take the warning...had to lure her to Vegas. But, Jack got careless with the body. Should have dumped it in the desert or near the A-bomb blast site..

-Anyone else? Let's make this a full confession

-Maybe.

-Why, Gordon? Why kill them?

-Lorraine's memory about her time at the Cooper's was starting to click in. I couldn't take the chance that she wouldn't confide her suspicions to her sister, April and you, shamus.

-What suspicions?

-About missing time. About killing the Cooper with an assist from their own son.

-Tom Cooper killed his own parents? I don't believe it.

-You don't want to believe it. I did the actual killing while Tom kept the girls occupied with the wonders of the forest. He pretended to be calling out to me; playing hide and seek It worked.

-Why kill them? They were going to adopt you, weren't they?

-No. At first, yes...but they started to wonder about me. Thought I was a little too strange for their suburban lifestyle. I knew they had money. Tom's old man was some kind of hot shot investment banker. His mother was an accountant. They lived this middle class life, but they didn't have to. It was all for show. I think maybe Mr. Cooper was an embezzler. When I found out that they weren't going to take me into the family fold...well, it kinda' forced me to take action. You know how it goes: survival of the fittest.

Edward was incredulous.

-And, Tom agreed to this?

-I bullied him into it. It was easy. I told him all we had to do was wait for the inheritance; just a few years. But, Tom didn't tell me he had grandparents who were gonna' take him in. I thought he'd be in the foundling home with me. I kept in touch, though, and threatened him. If I went down, so would he and maybe even more so.

-And, Lorraine? What was her part in all this?

-None...if you're talking about the urn. She was working for Romo-Ark. I think they were training her to be a sort of modern day Mata Hari. She probably would've been good at it, too. I ran into her. I was part of the Security Squad.

-What about those books on sound and vibration Lorraine had taken out of the library? What was her interest in them...or yours?

-I don't know what the hell you're talking about, man. I don't read technical books. I play with guns and people's lives. I'm good at that. Maybe, Lorraine had another boyfriend. She played around, you know.

Gordon Prentiss looked at his watch.

-Almost time.

-Gordon...don't do this.

-What have I got to lose?

-Your friggin' humanity, man.

-This was your father's idea. You know that, don't you?

-Not to murder innocent people.

-He taught me well. Took me under his wing and taught me all the tricks of black magic. Helped get me into Romo-Ark.

-How? How do you do it?

-Didn't your old man tell you? Focus your thought...visualize the target and place the urn-

Gordon Prentiss stopped smiling. The sound of police sirens could be heard in the distance.

-You're a bastard, Mendez.

-And, you're straight out of the gutter.

Edward jumped forward and kicked the urn into the black space behind Prentiss.

-You fool!

-Stand up. You're finished. Just-

Edward stopped in mid-sentence. The floor was shifting beneath his feet. He lost his balance and fell to the ground, but still holding on to his gun.

Gordon Prentiss, who had been sitting, got to his feet in spite of the tremor, turned about and looked for the urn. He couldn't find it in the darkness.

Edward regained his footing as Prentiss ran past him and up the plank staircase. The P. I. ran after him, but Prentiss had slammed the door shut and locked it from the outside. Edward shot the lock off, ran through the house and out the front door just in time to see Prentiss pull out of the driveway. Edward got into his DeSoto and gave chase. The three police cars that had come as back-up followed Edward's DeSoto.

The chase was on: five cars playing at it. Edward didn't think that Prentiss was armed, but he was dangerous. If he knew the black arts like he bragged, then he had to be stopped and put in prison.

In a few moments, the five cars emerged from the Holland Tunnel.

-The urn! Damn it! I hope it stays wherever the hell I kicked it. Can't think of that now. He's heading south toward the Brooklyn Bridge.

Gordon Prentiss was in a panic. He didn't know where he was going. His one plan had been wrecked. But, he knew that he had to get out of Manhattan. He was almost at the foot of the Brooklyn Bridge when his car started slowing down. He was out of gas. He cursed at the car...at Edward Mendez...and every deity that he could think of.

Prentiss got out of his car and headed toward the pedestrian walkway. Edward pulled his car over and went after him.

-Gordon, give it up.

Edward could hear the three police cars pulling up. He was catching up to Prentiss. He drew his revolver and shot Prentiss in the leg.

-You bastard!

Prentiss turned about and almost collided with Edward. The two men fell to the ground in hand to hand combat. Edward grabbed Prentiss by the collar, straightened him up and landed a right hook. Prentiss staggered back with blood streaming down his right leg. Edward had his Waltham pointed straight at him.

-It's over, Gordon.

-For once, we agree. I've killed without regret and guess what? I'm gonna' die that way. No one's gonna' burn me, man. No one.

And, without warning, Gordon Prentiss leaped to his death off the Brooklyn Bridge.

The police officers caught up to Edward. They looked on as Prentiss' body hit the water...killing him on impact.

-We'll get a patrol boat out there.

-No hurry. He's a goner.

-They'll want a body to confirm that, Mr. Mendez.

Edward turned away from the water below.

-The urn. It's back at Cooper's house. It's gotta be retrieved and destroyed.

The police officer didn't know what the P. I. was talking about.

-It's okay, Officer. I'll pick it up. And, then, I think we've got some red tape to get through.

-Mr. Mendez, I guess you haven't heard.

-Heard what?

-It just came through from the 86th.

-What came through, Officer?

But, the P. I. had a gut feeling that he already knew.

-Your father is dead. He died of a heart attack in the Emergency Room at Wyckoff Hospital. I'm sorry.

-So am I, Officer. So am I.

EPILOGUE

-THE URN'S been destroyed, Marlena. It went into the furnace at a refining plant in Jersey. I threw it into the furnace myself.

-I imagine that it was necessary, but how does one cope with such a loss?

-A loss, mother?

-Yes. But, I wonder...was a signal sent to that ancient race?

-We'll never know, will we?

Edward lit a Lucky Strike and smiled warmly at Susan.

-I hope not, Susan.

-What do you mean, dear boy?

-I've got a real bad feeling about this ancient race. Better not to have any contact. We've gotten along this far without them.

-So, you believe that they exist.

-I'd bet money on it, Marlena.

Susan suppressed a shiver.

-Just thinking about it gives me the creeps. It's a frightening prospect.. making contact with a race of beings from another planet. I agree with Edward about them.

Marlena changed the subject.

-So, Edward, the Lorraine Keyes murder has been cleared up?

-Prentiss murdered her and Miss Matthews. A man named Jack Dana killed April out in Vegas. We'll never know the entire motive, but he had to cover up his crime of fifteen years ago: the murder of Gordon Cooper's parents.

-How did your father's path and Prentiss' cross?

The P. I took a drag on his cigarette and shrugged his broad shoulders.

-No idea...not really. Prentiss and my father had contacts with Romo-Ark. It doesn't matter. They're both dead.

Susan got up to get another drink. Edward noticed how nervous she was.

-Susan? You okay? You look kind of rattled.

-Not really. I'm still thinking of that alien race and Professor Bennett. I don't know which gives me the shivers more. There's something insidious about that man.

Susan had told Edward about the revelation she had had concerning Professor Bennett.

-The unknown is always frightening. As for Professor Bennett, that's another mystery in itself. I wonder why he was prowling around here that night. Was it just for the urn?

-Or for something else? But, what else could it be?

That was Marlena who asked that question.

Again, Edward shrugged.

-I think I just might ask him next time I see him. What have I got to lose?

Susan got back to the previous subject.

-Edward, you don't think that this alien race is among us now, do you? Please say "no."

-Hadn't thought of that, but...

He took a drag on his cigarette.

-...you never know.

NEXT:

EGYPT: THE LAST SUNRISE

AN EDWARD MENDEZ, P. I. THRILLER
BOOK XI

ABOUT THE AUTHOR

Gerard Denza has worked in the Publicity Dept. of Random House and Little, Brown, and Company in New York City. He's worked with such authors as Pete Hamill, Willie Morris, Pat Booth and Arthur C. Clarke.

He is also the playwright and director of several Off-Off Broadway plays which include:

Icarus

Mahler: The Man Who Was Never Born

The Dying God: A Vampire's Tale

Shadows Behind the Footlights

The Housedress

His noir play, **Edmond: The Likely**, has been recorded for radio broadcast.

Mr. Denza is a graduate of Fordham University where he majored in Psychology and graduated Magna Cum Laude. He is hard at work on his next **Edward Mendez, P. I. Thriller** novel.

Made in the USA
Coppell, TX
29 March 2024